# THE SOVEREIGN AMERICAN

## By

### Howard L. Moxham

### Copyright 2003

ISBN 0-7414-1679-4

*Published by:*

PUBLISHING.COM

*519 West Lancaster Avenue*
*Haverford, PA 19041-1413*
*Info@buybooksontheweb.com*
*www.buybooksontheweb.com*
*Toll-free (877) BUY BOOK*
*Local Phone (610) 520-2500*
*Fax (610) 519-0261*

*Printed in the United States of America*

*Printed on Recycled Paper*

*Published  August 2003*

# CONTENTS

INTRODUCTION ..................................................................................i

CHAPTER 1 .........................................................................................1
CHAPTER 2 Definitions of Importance .............................................4
CHAPTER 3 How Much Government? ..............................................6
CHAPTER 4 The UN and the CFR ...................................................11
CHAPTER 5 The CFR and the Trilateral Commission ....................13
CHAPTER 6 Democrats and Republicans.........................................15
CHAPTER 7 Our Outlaw Federal Judiciary.....................................17
CHAPTER 8 American Citizenship ..................................................20
CHAPTER 9 Patriotism and Allegiance...........................................22
CHAPTER 10 Arms and the American Citizen..................................24
CHAPTER 11 Freedom and Sovereignty .........................................26
CHAPTER 12 Revolution - It was our Genesis -
       It will be our Rebirth! ...............................................28
CHAPTER 13 The New Declaration of Independence of 2002 .........30
CHAPTER 14 The Words of Our Greatest President ........................37
CHAPTER 15 Who Are The Members of the CFR? ..........................39
CHAPTER 16 Domestic Enemies .....................................................41
CHAPTER 17 Globalism and You ....................................................43
CHAPTER 18 The Presidency............................................................46
CHAPTER 19 The Dangers of Gradualism and the Future ..............48
CHAPTER 20 The Cost of Changing Governments...........................50
CHAPTER 21 The Constitution of the United States ........................52
CHAPTER 22 Proposed Changes in The Constitution......................54
CHAPTER 23 How Corporations Expand Their Power
       and Influence.........................................................84
CHAPTER 24 Are we Morally Bankrupt? ........................................86
CHAPTER 25 The World Bank and IMF...........................................88
CHAPTER 26 The Political Left and Right........................................90
CHAPTER 27 The Propagandists......................................................92
CHAPTER 28 The Separation of Church And State .........................94
CHAPTER 29 What Happened to the FBI And CIA? .......................96
CHAPTER 30 How The American People Will Change
       America Forever ....................................................98
ABOUT THE FUTURE ..................................................................104
APPENDIX 1 The Truth About Nuclear War .................................105
APPENDIX 2 After the Attack - How do we Survive? ..................121
APPENDIX 3 Supporting Data ......................................................127

# INTRODUCTION

Two Hundred and twenty six years ago, in 1776, our forefathers, after years of deprivations and conflict with the despotic king of England, revolted, and at the Second Continental Congress declared that the 13 original colonies, were thereafter free and independent states.

To formalize and legalize their new status, free of England's punitive laws and misdeeds, they created the Declaration of Independence, our most important Founding document. It revealed before the world the many misdeeds and usurpations of the king and the powerful ministers of his Government, and declared that England would have no further control over the Colonies. It also declared that whenever the Government no longer served the people, they should throw off that Government and replace it with one that serves the people. Indeed, it admonished, and required that the people act to change their Government to assure their own future.

Thus was born a Government "of the people, by the people and for the people", which Abraham Lincoln so clearly described in his Gettysburg address, 87 years later. His fear was that that form of Government would "disappear from the face of the earth". As you know, it survived the Civil War, but since WW II has become more and more in danger of elimination. It is the opinion of the Sovereign American that forces in Washington and New York are behind this attack on our freedoms.

After the signing of the Declaration of Independence, war with England's armies was ongoing, and continued until British General Cornwallis was defeated by General George Washington at Yorktown, Virginia, in 1781. The war of Independence was finally over.

Our forefathers believed that Government must be restrained to prevent misdeeds and attempts to impoverish, enslave or overpower the people. To assure that the people would be protected from such Government, they created the Constitution of the United States. The Constitution operates to tell the Government how it can function in support of the people. It limits the functions of the Government. And, the Constitution also elicited the rights of the people, which were unalienable and derived from the almighty. The first ten Amendments to the Constitution, the Bill of Rights, resulted.

Our forefathers would not permit a king in this country, believing that any sovereign would eventually become a despot and they would be no better off than they had been under the King of England. They therefore, in the Declaration of Independence, made every citizen of the United States a sovereign in his own right and armed him with the 2nd Amendment to the Constitution to assure his continued control over Government.

Today, hundreds of years later, we face not the king of England but our own Government, which for a half-century has become increasingly unconstitutional in its actions, precisely the problem the framers of the Constitution and the Declaration of Independence feared would happen. It is clear to many Americans that the time is approaching when we must change our Government, or it will be so entrenched, behind so many "laws" that it will be impossible to change. But Government will resist change that it does not initiate. That is the modern conundrum.

The Sovereign American is dedicated to revealing the unconstitutional actions of the Government. This is especially true of an Oligarchy, a Government of the intelligentsia, the wealthy aristocracy that has high jacked our Government, and therefore our lives. This cabal is known as the Council on Foreign Relations.

You might think, from its name, that it is a Government agency. It is not. It is a secret, private organization of extremely wealthy and dangerous aristocrats that has penetrated our Government to an unprecedented degree.

Who runs the CFR? David Rockefeller, the grandson of the infamous and hated robber baron of years past. He is following his grandfather's example with a vengeance. The

CFR and its sister organization, The Trilateral Commission, are the most dangerous organizations in the world today. Who runs the Trilateral Commission? None other than David Rockefeller!

Why is the CFR dangerous? Because their activities work against the American people and their ability to control their Government. Americans are fast losing control over not only their Government, but their future. Something must be done.

# CHAPTER 1

In times of strife and war, it is extremely difficult to publish commentary which is critical in any way of the Government of our country. Every instinct in Americans is to support the Government in such times. Yet, there is no requirement for any free American to remain silent when great danger for our Republic lurks within the Government itself and its policies, especially in time of War.

The Sovereign American is dedicated to exposing these hazards, because the history of our Government in the twentieth century is that devious, even subversive actions are undertaken while the attention of the people is diverted away from Government. Wartime is the essential time to critically observe what the Government is doing behind the scenes. If you can find out. That's the rub. And that's why the Sovereign American is being published.

The Sovereign American is dedicated also to reminding those Citizens among us that our Forefathers, at great hazard to their lives, created a land of the free, where every person is a Sovereign. We have no King in America, no sovereign leader. Our Forefathers distrusted any and all Sovereign heads of Government in any land. To prevent a despotic leader coming to the fore in the United States, they created instead, a land where the people hold the full power of the Government in their hands. Americans temporarily allow a Government to lead them, but they can change that Government at any time, election or not. If conditions become intolerable for the average person, direct action can be taken to change the Government. Every American alive today must realize that fact. It will become increasingly important in the coming years. Much must be done. And time is running short.

Whatever Americans do, there are two things they must always keep in their minds and hearts, and they are passages from our Founding Documents. The Declaration of Independence and the Constitution of the United States:

From the Declaration of Independence, the most important of our Founding Documents, because without it there would have been no basis for the Constitution and the Bill of Rights:

"...."that to secure these rights Governments are instituted among men, deriving their just powers from the consent of the governed, that when any form of Government becomes destructive of these ends, it is the right of the people to alter or abolish it, and to institute new Government....'

And from the Constitution itself:

"We the people of the United States, in order to form a more perfect union, establish justice, insure domestic tranquility, provide for the common defense, promote the general welfare, and secure the blessings of liberty to ourselves and our posterity..."

These basics in our Founding Documents apply to the United States and its citizens, not to other lands and other peoples, and not to the millions of illegal aliens living in the United States. It is the contention of the Sovereign American that the Government has failed many tests entailed in those documents, and has for many years embarked on a deliberate plan to marginalize and render impotent and unimportant the very words and meaning of the Constitution. The Sovereign American holds that such actions of the Government are themselves a violation of the Constitution and the trust that the people must have in their Government. From that trust derives consent. And consent is paramount in the American scheme of Government. Without the consent of the people, Government has no authority.

Some Americans and many foreigners, including those in power, sometimes delude themselves that America and Americans are soft and too used to the easy life to fight for their rights, or to defend the country. The Japanese made that mistake in 1941 when they attacked Pearl Harbor in Hawaii, far from the Continental United States. The result was that we practically destroyed Japan, and made a parking lot of their major cities. And we helped millions of them join their ancestors in their own version of the hereafter. And damned few Americans were upset about that fact.

Germany, too, thought they were superior to us in 1941, and they declared war on us thinking that the Americans were just another kind of Britons. Not likely. Germans, the most similar people to Americans in Europe, and masters of technology, had never seen anyone fight a war as we did. We overwhelmed them in every respect. And the German fighting machine was the world's best. But they fell just the same. They feared the Russians more than us, because they knew the Russians would slaughter them given the opportunity to do so, but they feared no such reaction from the Americans. We were too civilized to slaughter them once they had surrendered. But Germany was destroyed almost completely in the end. And the human cost was unspeakable.

The world had learned a tough lesson. Screw the Americans and you'd better duck, because the kitchen sink is on the way. The world has to be reminded of that fact every generation or so.

# CHAPTER 2

## DEFINITIONS OF IMPORTANCE

To understand what is happening to our Government, and therefore our nation, the average person needs to brush up on several important terms that affect his or her daily life:

**A Cabal**-A Cabal is a collection of a few people who plot (usually secretly) to change the Government to that which they deem correct or which meets their needs.

**An Oligarchy**- A form of Government in which the power to govern is vested in a few.

**A Monarchy**- A form of Government which is ruled by a Monarch, a King.

**An Aristocracy**- A Government in which the privileged class, usually by lineage, holds power.

**A Plutocracy**- Rule by the rich. A ruling class of the wealthy.

**World Government**- A Government superior to all Governments around the world, and which they would have to obey, regardless of their people's wishes.

All of the above forms of Government are unconstitutional and therefore illegal in the United States of America. However, The Council on Foreign Relations (CFR) is an organization that fits the description of a Cabal, Oligarchy, Plutocracy or Aristocracy. The CFR is not a Government organization, but is a collection of so-called aristocrats who are extremely wealthy, and who operate in secrecy to control the Government of the United States.

**A Republic**- A form of Government where the powers of the Government are widely delegated to the people. In the United States, The Declaration of Independence delegated the powers of the Government directly to the people, but are temporarily transferred to Representatives of the people at the seat of Government. Government of the people, by the people, for the people.

**A Democracy-** Government by the people. Marked by dissension and factionalism. This word does not appear in any of our Founding Documents.

**A Renegade-** One who throws off allegiance to embrace another, usually opposed. A defector, or betrayer.

**A Tergiversator-** One who changes his allegiance. Unreliable. A renegade.

**Tergiversation-** The act of changing allegiance, usually to the opposite of once held beliefs.

**Xenophobia-** A fear or dislike of strangers or Foreigners.

# CHAPTER 3

## HOW MUCH GOVERNMENT?

How much Government do Americans believe we need? Do we need the monstrous Government that has metastasized in Washington over the past fifty years? Of course not. But it is the nature of politics, politicians and bureaucrats to build and defend turf. It is not their fault, in their view, that more and more Government costs more and more money. More and more taxes. It is obvious that no one has been looking after your financial well being in those fifty years. Politicians and bureaucrats have never seen a tax they did not like.

Government and politicians need to learn that Government is not free to do whatever it likes in this country, and around the world. The Constitution is in place to limit Government. Politicians and bureaucrats do not like to be limited in anything they do, and therefore often look askance at the Constitution, if they look at all. It is small leap to unconstitutional actions. A leap that most politicians make with alacrity.

Everyone knows that it is practically impossible to fire Government employees. Their jobs are recession- and depression-proof. No federal employee is ever laid off, even in times of contraction. This is the fault of the Congress. They write the laws that protect even the most inept and stupid workers of the Government. This is a perfect example of why we need term limits for Congressmen and Senators.

Many things the Government does today are unconstitutional. We need much less Government and much less taxes to support it. Originally, tariffs on foreign goods brought here for sale to Americans paid for the entire federal budget. Americans paid nothing to support the Government. Originally there were no federal income taxes. Americans kept everything they earned in wages. There were no withholding taxes. And all America prospered.

How do you think the great cities and industries of America came into being? It was because for a century the American people were not saddled with confiscatory taxes, big Government with massive programs that extended all over the world, and a military that did not consume the wealth of the people. But during WW II big Government and globalization reversed our historic stance. All of these costs are now borne by Americans. A system of tariffs and access fees must be reinstated in this country. We need to junk the Export/Import bank. We need to junk subsidies for large corporations to advertise and sell their wares overseas.

Even though we are capitalists, and believe in that system implicitly, there are changes that are needed. Unbridled capitalism becomes predatory. We need to institute laws that will cap the growth of corporations at 100 million dollars. Unrestricted growth of corporations gives them too much wealth and too much power, here and abroad. We need to dismantle the IMF and World Bank, and all international free trade agreements that work against the American citizen. And we need to stop immediately the free flow of capital around the world, which benefits no one but the International Bankers and large corporations. In other words, the American people need to take charge of their Government.

The American people are on the verge of a classic struggle with Government. Who is going to control this country? Unrestricted and all-powerful Government, unrestricted and all-powerful corporations, with the people unable to say no, enough is enough? Or are the people going to resist more and more Government, no matter what the cost is to them? And make no mistake, a despotic and all-powerful Government can wreak terrible vengeance on those who would resist, just as a despotic and all powerful corporation can wreak terrible penalties on its employees. Today, they are one and the same. No matter, the struggle must begin, and soon. Voting does not help. No matter who you elect, he is part of the problem, because the two political parties control those who run. How do you think George W.

Bush amassed millions of dollars when he began his run for the Presidency? The answer is obvious to everyone. Large and powerful corporations, wealthy bankers and international financiers, etc. The Democrats are no different, they have access to multi-million dollar donors as well. These people are not interested in change. But change they must.

Government will dictate how difficult the coming struggle will be, and how it will be fought. They will dictate how resistance will be dealt with. History says that it will not be pretty. But we have no choice if we intend to remain free and in charge of our own constitutional future, and that of our children and grandchildren. We dare not give up. We must not give up. We will not give up. Our forefathers gave us the Declaration of Independence which requires us to act, as the sole Sovereigns in this land.

The change in Government must be peaceful, as is our tradition. This is not a call to arms for the various Militias, who have been grossly maligned by the media, and whose members have largely gone underground. It is not a call for the violent overthrow of the Government. It is a call for all Americans to consider where we are headed. It is a call for an intellectual revolution seeking to change our Government. Enough people of the same mind can make the changes necessary, and without violence.

Nevertheless, the Government will dictate whether the change is violent or not. Overblown politicians and bureaucrats will want to hold on to their jobs and will use every Government police and enforcement agency to stop the change. That is natural, but it flies in the face of what must happen. It is their decision to stand aside or try to fight against the rising tide that will eventually drown them. That is not our way. It should not be theirs.

Change must come, for the future is clear. More and more Government unconstitutional actions will eventually overwhelm the people and their will to resist. They will count on the use of every dirty trick and widespread media ridicule to initially oppose change and those who propose it. That is a tried and true method liberals and their kissing cousins, the communists and socialists have used around the world to fight those who would challenge them. The Government of the United States will show us its true stripes when that time comes. First ridicule, then the full weight of the law, and eventually armed force. It is then that the people will realize just how little our Government is dedicated to the Declaration of Independence and the Constitution.

How will change be made? Given the demonstrated callousness and iron hand of Washington, only large numbers of people demonstrating for change will work. LARGE numbers. Simultaneous demonstrations must take place in cities across this land, including Washington. A massive letter writing campaign should precede the demonstrations.

Your Congressman and Senator would rather eat dirt than face a determined citizen in his office, let alone a dozen, but that is precisely where you must go. He or she will do nothing, but the effect of these actions will be whispered about in the cloakrooms and furtive glances at their contemporaries will certainly result. Eventually, confrontations will take place, and they are critical to both sides. Steel nerves will be required, and gritted teeth. If we are lucky, violence will be avoided, but this will only happen if those in Washington begin to accede to the wishes of the people.

And what if the people are successful? There is no immediate need to rewrite the Constitution although it does need to be changed. Many of the needed changes in our Government can be made by a new Congress and by action of a determined new President. But new elections must be held as soon as possible to seat the new Congress. And the Constitution must be upheld, even though the rejected politicians and bureaucrats must be prevented from running for office or positions of influence in the new Government. This will be the greatest challenge for the new Government but it must be done.

There will be changes necessary in the Constitution to ensure that politicians and bureaucrats cannot again reinstate what they were doing before the change in Government. In fact, the new Government should not hold a Constitutional Convention until much later. Why? The new Convention will be a magnet for the rejected politicians and bureaucrats of the old Government, and they must not be permitted to infect the new Government. To be absolutely certain of the will of the people, the new Constitutional Convention should be delayed until most of the old Government employees and officials have passed. It will require patience, but unless it can be assured that the snake will not rise again, haste is not desired. Change, yes, permanent changes, but in time.

We do not change our Government, as the Declaration of Independence says, for light or transient causes, but for the protection of our nation and our society. And for our children and grandchildren, and theirs as well. Once in two hundred twenty-six years proves that. But our Government has been high jacked and taken over by ruthless wealthy men in Washington and New York. They must be cast out and vilified, and the people must regain control of their Government. We have no other choice, if we are to remain free Americans.

# CHAPTER 4

## THE UNITED NATIONS & THE COUNCIL ON FOREIGN RELATIONS

Two organizations in the world hold much danger for the people and Government of the United States. Both are extremely dangerous. The first is the United Nations (UN), and the second is the Council on Foreign Relations (CFR). The United Nations is a dagger aimed at the heart of the United States, its Constitution, its Declaration of Independence and its citizens and their Sovereignty. It is the first hazard because it is organized and represented throughout the world. The second, the CFR, is as much or more dangerous as the UN, because it operates in secrecy, behind the scenes. It is a Cabal of millionaires and multi-millionaires, with no more than 4000 odd members, but because of the immense wealth of its founders and directors, its influence is breath-taking.

The United Nations is a collection of ne'erdo wells, and bureaucrats from its member nations. The functions and objectives of the UN are incompatible with the laws and future of the United States, for it ostensibly is to become a world Government supreme over all nations, which will be subservient to its directives and control. The Sovereignty of each nation is of no concern to the UN and is considered to be an outmoded concept. Indeed, a former Attorney General of the United States publicly stated in the year 2000 that this was true. Naturally, no one is asking the American people what their views are on the matter.

Persons adhering to such sentiments either do not remember or understand that the Founders of the Republic, in the Declaration of Independence, invested the rights of a Sovereign with the individual American. Each American is a Sovereign in his own right, so that when the uneducated or those who advocate the end of Sovereignty in America, they are really attacking the right of individual Americans to control their own future, their own Government. No one, foreigner or mistaken American, can make that change stick. If they try to do so, a conflagration will ensue.

It is with great concern that most Americans finally realize that their own Government, during wartime in 1945 established the UN and began the subversive and unconstitutional acts that set the country on a course for eventual world Government that would supersede and render impotent the sovereignty of the United States. The beginnings of the UN and all its subordinate organizations, at the behest of the CFR, were the darkest days in the history of the United States. Those days marked the beginning of the loss of control the American people had over their own Government. That control has never been restored. But the people will yet prevail.

The essential thing to remember about the United Nations and its super Government is that the whole concept is unconstitutional and therefore illegal in the United States. And the concept of a private, secret organization of millionaires taking over the United States Government is just as unconstitutional and illegal. Yet that is precisely what they have done. And that is what you must fight. Do you see a parallel with 1945?

# CHAPTER 5

## THE COUNCIL ON FOREIGN RELATIONS & THE TRILATERAL COMMISSION

The Council on Foreign Relations is a private, secret organization that has existed since the First World War But it remained relatively dormant for years, until World War II, when it was directed toward new goals by David Rockefeller.

Why is the organization labeled a secret one? First, its members are forbidden, on pain of expulsion, to reveal the subjects covered, and opinions expressed, in any of their meetings, to outsiders, particularly the press. Second, its annual meetings are closed to the public. Third, their members must be nominated for membership by an existing member. Outsiders may not apply. It is truly an organization of wealthy elitists.

The CFR is a Cabal, some would say a Cartel, with no more than 4000 odd members, but practically every major Corporation in the US is a member, and supports it financially. Incidentally, 4000 members out of a US population of more than 260 million people certainly qualifies it as a Cabal, and it certainly operates like a Trust. (A Trust you will remember is a combine of organizations operating under the direction of a single leadership, while a Cartel is a collection of organizations operating on their own. A Cabal is distinguished by its plotting to change Government or control Government. Take your choice; they are all unconstitutional and illegal in the United States.)

The CFR is responsible for the entire globalization program undertaken since WW II by the Government. How did this occur? In preparation for the execution of this undertaking, and others, members of the CFR were placed in most departments of the Government by not an electoral process, but by appointment. Presidents who were members of the CFR made the appointments. Members of the CFR assisted the Chief Executive in making the selections by nominating or suggesting appointees. Most or all of the selectees were installed without approval of Congress. This process has continued for nearly fifty years, until now there are many appointees in the Government, all speaking with one voice. Voices which parrot the CFR line on any subject.

The Trilateral Commission was founded in 1973 by David Rockefeller. While the CFR is made up of approximately 4000 citizens of the United States, the Trilateral Commission is made up of foreign politicians, bankers, industrialists, and so on. The trilateral refers to Europe, North America and the Pacific Rim countries (originally Japan), but now includes China. One major purpose of the CFR is to influence legislation through the US Congress that will aid the other countries mentioned as well as trilateral objectives.

The effectiveness of the CFR and Trilateral plans have resulted in an amazing control over international markets, previously controlled by sovereign countries. The CFR and the Trilateral Trust now controls most world markets and the trade flowing between most nations of the earth. In addition, they control almost totally the flow of capital around the world. This amounts to more than a trillion dollars a day in the US alone.

All of this was envisioned in the mind of David Rockefeller, who put it all together and made it work. His grandfather, John D. Rockefeller, the vicious robber baron of the early twentieth century, must be chortling in glee from his grave. Old John D. merely bludgeoned his way to complete control over the US oil industry-David has captured the US Government and the entire world of commerce and finance. It truly runs in the family. God help the little guy.

# CHAPTER 6

## DEMOCRATS & REPUBLICANS

The two major political parties, the Republicans and Democrats are now so thoroughly corrupt that no matter which one is the winner in an election, nothing will change. Although change is what the people want, they are frustrated by the fact that the same philosophical views control each party. Free Trade, Globalization, NAFTA, GATT, the United Nations, etc.

Further, the two national parties control the candidates who shall run, the discourse that shall take place between the parties and the number of candidates that shall participate in any national debates. In other words, no outsiders need apply. The affect of this arrangement is clear. There shall be no changes made, no matter what the people think or want. This is not what the Founding Fathers had in mind in 1797, when they created this great nation. In fact, the Founding Fathers would probably hang most politicians from the lamp posts of Washington if they were alive today because of the damage they have done to representative Government.

The essential thing that must be remembered about the Democrats is that they are Socialists. The Socialists around the world have been cast onto the trash heap of history, but looney American liberals have not learned that as yet. But they should all remember that two more prominent Socialists nearly destroyed Europe in the last century. They were Adolph Hitler, and Josef Stalin, a dedicated National Socialist and a dedicated communist, the head of the Union of Soviet Socialist Republics (USSR).

The Republicans are no better. They are dedicated totally to their brand of Capitalism. That is to say that they believe that Corporations are an entity created by God, and no one less than a millionaire should be treated as an equal let alone a member of Congress. Exclusivity is the hallmark of their credo.

It has been obvious for decades that neither political party is for the average American. Nothing will change in the Government as long as no other real political choice exists. A developing and burgeoning third party is essential for the future well-being of the Republic. Continuation of the philosophy of Government adopted by the Republicans and Democrats will destroy the Republic which our forefathers gave us. We cannot permit that to happen.

The Senate. How can a body of politicians, half of whom are millionaires, function to represent states or the people? They can't. They have little understanding of the life the average person lives, they have nothing in common with the people. But they have a lot in common with other millionaires and the elitists with whom they interact.

The House of Representatives. Although the problem of millionaires is less acute in the House, money is a major problem. Most Representatives never saw a handout they didn't like. Love is perhaps a more appropriate word. In other words they are for sale.

Are there any good people in the House and Senate? Of course, but they are far outnumbered by those who should be purged from the Capitol forever.

# CHAPTER 7

## OUR OUTLAW FEDERAL JUDICIARY

We have among our leaders in Washington, an elitist Supreme Court. It is called the Supreme Court because our forefathers wanted the law of the land to be in the hands of a court to reign over all courts in the land. It is not named that because of any special qualities the members of the court might possess. Yet our "Supremes" work only part of the year. They loaf the rest of the time. And they are in the court for life.

One can easily understand why these outlaws see themselves as special persons. They need to be given a lesson in humility. Why are they outlaws? It is simple. They "interpret" the words of the Constitution, as if none of the people can read for themselves what the Constitution says. No matter, they have for years "interpreted" their way into new and obscure readings of one of our most sacred documents. And in doing so they have created new laws, which is none of their business.

The Court has abandoned one of the most important tenets of our Nation. Abraham Lincoln espoused it perfectly in the Gettysburg Address on November 19, 1863. He said, among other things, that "Government of the people, by the people and for the people, shall not perish from this earth..." The Supreme Court to its everlasting shame substituted its treasonous view that the people no longer matter. Corporations matter. Power matters. Their actions are therefore unconstitutional. All that matters in this country are the people. The People. Any court decision that works against the people is unconstitutional.

The federal judiciary, in the lower courts, have on many occasions "overruled' and nullified elections by the people. They have forced new taxes on the people, in violation of the Constitution. The "Supreme" Court remains silent on these activists in robes. The Florida Supreme Court, full of political activists, attempted to influence the 2000 election in favor of a Democrat presidential candidate. They were overruled by the Supreme Court in a controversial decision which clouded the national election and the election of a new president. Yet the cause of the controversy was the actions of the Florida Supreme court.

Even higher Courts are not immune from the lunacy that now infects our Judiciary. The Ninth Circuit Court has decided that the Pledge of Allegiance is unconstitutional. This is a direct result of loony Liberals sitting on the courts. Liberals of all stripes are the destroyers of tradition, the destructors of long held values on the part of the public and the authors of Political Correctness. Their very presence in the Nation is an abomination. They must be purged from the court system to prevent them from further damaging our Nation.

The Constitution declares the Supreme Court members shall be on the bench for life. This must change, or there must be a more definitive clarification of the "good behavior" clause of the Constitution. Activism on the part of any Court cannot be permitted to continue.

The most serious offense of all is that several members of the Supreme Court have disqualified themselves to sit on the court by becoming members of the Council on Foreign Relations. Their membership causes them to be in violation of their oaths of office and renders their decisions in any case before it involving suits against the CFR to be null and void. Any such suit brought against the CFR cannot be fairly judged by the court with sitting members of the court so clearly in conflict with their duties. It is clear that these members are on the bench to protect the interests of the CFR, and not to serve justice.

Where will plaintiffs go for relief? The answer is obvious. Nowhere. The Supreme Court must be cleansed, and their members prohibited from joining any group which is dedicated to changing the Government to their liking.

To rectify the usurpations of the Court, which has eliminated the "one man one vote" proposition from our laws, in favor of one of their infamous "interpretations", where "wealth equals free speech," or "one corporation, many votes", the Court must be rejected and replaced with a peoples court.

Until that day, the Supreme Court must be required to spend its leisure time reviewing laws passed by the Congress before they become laws instead of taking months off from their jobs. They must be required to work the same way the average Citizen works.

And, as there is no requirement in the Constitution for the judges of the Supreme Court to be lawyers, a majority of the members must in the future be average citizens. The people must rule where the Supreme Court goes, not lawyers, the most untrustworthy group in the land. Indeed, the Supreme Court must be renamed The Peoples Supreme Court. Only then will the people begin to reclaim their Government. The People. THE PEOPLE! The people are what count in this nation, and the Supreme Court must be held accountable to that premise.

And finally, the Supreme Court must be restrained in its judgments. Instead of handing down decisions on approximately 80 cases per year, the court must be limited to no more than six cases per year. As long as the court hears enough cases to hand down 80 decisions, that means that approximately 3.5 days are devoted to each case. This is certainly thin devotion to the Constitution and cannot be called justice.

# CHAPTER 8

## AMERICAN CITIZENSHIP

Most Americans are as firmly Citizens of the United States as our forefathers were. It would be unthinkable for most Americans to be citizens of another Government or nation. Yet we have among us, some Americans who are turncoats or renegades. They have an Allegiance to a nascent World Government, the United Nations. They are tergiversators, an ugly word that fittingly, denotes those who have changed their allegiance to another Government.

Since the United Nations believes itself to be, and intends to be a world Government, (Unconstitutional in the United States), supporters of the United Nations are confessed turncoats, who have rejected the United States as their Government. A betrayal so repugnant that most Americans would die before making that choice. Since every member of the Council on Foreign Relations and American members of the Trilateral Commission, subscribes to those organization's objective, which is the establishment of a world Government through the United Nations, they are confessed turncoats. Tergiversators. They do not deserve to be Americans, and in fact cannot claim to be Americans. A Bill of Attainder must be issued by the Congress and their citizenship must be forfeit. They deserve the penalties that status implies. Further, since the objectives of the United Nations include elimination of the Constitutional rights now enjoyed by Americans, they must be charged with treason, for they are giving aid and comfort to an enemy state. Finally, since they are no longer are Americans, they must be deported, for their residence here is a hazard to the Republic which they have abandoned and an insult to all loyal Americans.

If that seems harsh, our own President has stated, if you are not with us you are against us, or words to that effect. Tergiversators cannot have it both ways. In addition to being turncoats and traitors, they are Domestic Enemies, for they no longer believe in or support the Constitution of the United States. Truly they are the ugliest of Americans.

The Sovereign American has some advice for others who would emulate these characters. Be Americans or get the Hell out!

# CHAPTER 9

## PATRIOTISM AND ALLEGIANCE

Most Americans, who are not recent immigrants to the United States, feel their patriotism to their country deeply. Patriotism has become a dirty word for some in this country in recent years, and Liberal leftists, those originators and guardians of Political Correctness have even coined a relatively new word to shift the meaning away from its traditional definition. That word is Nationalism. It is used throughout the media and the world of higher education, to avoid the word they hate, Patriotism.

But try as they might, Liberals have been unable to extinguish the light of Patriotism in the American people. That was demonstrated immediately after the attacks on the World Trade Center in New York. Imagine the frustration of those Liberal leaders who saw thirty years work go down the drain in those terrible hours. If they were unaware of how far out of mainstream life their views are in this country that should lead them to understand that Liberalism, like its cousin, Socialism, is unwanted in this land.

Yet many Liberals, in their own squirrelly way, would be aghast at any suggestion that their allegiance might lie in any other Government than our own. Liberals, as bad as they are, are not the main problem. Others are.

Those who support the United Nations, including virtually every members of the Council on Foreign Relations and the American members of the Trilateral Commission are tergiversators. These people, who were American citizens, have more allegiance to a foreign political body, the United Nations, than the United States. As such, they are easily identified as Domestic Enemies.

One cannot have divided loyalties and be a patriotic American. Either your allegiance lies with the US or it does not. Such people should leave the United States and take up residence in another country. Otherwise their tergiversation should be cause for prosecution.

One can imagine the howls of indignation that would result from them at the suggestion that they are no longer patriotic Americans. Yet that is what they are. And they should get out of this country.

# CHAPTER 10

## ARMS AND THE AMERICAN CITIZEN

If you are aware of what our Government has been doing over the past few decades, you are aware that something is wrong. There is a skewing of the American dream that does not serve the American citizen well. In fact, the more time that passes, the more uncomfortable you will become. Millions of Americans are earning less than they did in the 1960's. This is not by chance; it is by design, because there are those in power in Washington and New York who value you less and less. You now are little better off than the millions of illegal aliens that infest our land and feed the ever increasing need of corporations for cheap labor. You are now, and have been since the late 1940's, under the control of the wealthy aristocracy that has stolen our Government.

Is there an end to this treadmill? Yes, complete subjugation. In the end, you will be no different than the downtrodden millions of South America, of Yugoslavia, of Russia, of Poland and of many other nations. They are virtually penniless and powerless. They have been downtrodden all their lives, because they cannot change their Governments to be more aligned with their needs. Representative Governments, republics, are not part of their lives, nor are written constitutions to protect their rights.

But even in poverty, you are an American. You are different. Your forefathers gave you the power, the duty, to change your Government when necessary for your own good. They made you a Sovereign. And they made you an armed Sovereign. The Government knows this and they fear you. They do not fear you as long as you are not armed. And that is why the attacks on the 2nd Amendment to the Constitution have become more and more strident in the past decade. If you ever hope to change your Government for the better, voting won't do it under current conditions, where a

24

third party is shut out completely, but the threat of armed uprising or secession will.

Accordingly, arms and the American Citizen are and should be, inseparable. That is the only thing that makes you different. You should recognize that fact, and accordingly, guard the 2nd Amendment fiercely. And guard your arms. You may need them.

# CHAPTER 11

## FREEDOM AND SOVEREIGNTY

Many in Government and the media believe that Americans of the twenty first century have lost their concern for their liberties and Sovereignty. Nothing could be further from the truth, for modern Americans know very well how much their lives depend on freedom.

One of the most puzzling of questions has been asked more and more frequently after 9-11-01, the date of the infamous attack on our country, is "How much freedom are you willing to give up?" supposedly in a trade-off for more security in our lives. How ridiculous! Americans are not going to give up ANY freedoms in the name of security or anything else.

This question is most often asked by newsmen, many of whom are among the least trustworthy of our citizens. They are invariably Democrats, but with an agenda which must be recognized by even the most casual observer. The wished for reply would of course be "a lot", for the questioner is really interested in changing America in ways that virtually every one of his listeners would reject out of hand.

Our freedoms mean much more to the average American than the Government or the sleazy politician or equally sleazy newsman believes. They believe that you are lazy and uncaring about your future, and with your acquiescence they will achieve their ends sooner than they thought, and with less resistance than they thought. Fat chance!

As for our Sovereignty, most Americans know that unless we run our own country, someone else will run it for us. They already know that we are on the edge of a precipice in that regard. Our own Government has made great progress toward embracing a so-called World Government. Powerful forces in Washington and New York are behind such Un-American beliefs, and they are ruthless in their battle to take away the most precious of rights that Americans possess. For Americans are their own Sovereigns, and they will give up that right on a cold day in Hell.

Eternal vigilance has always been the clarion call of patriots and the kind of patriots that the modern world has never seen lurk just under the horizon in America, and the very thought of what might happen terrifies those in power, for a fully aroused, armed populace is capable of destroying them without a second thought. That's why the sustained attacks on the Second Amendment were begun a decade ago and are continuing. Eternal vigilance is more necessary now than ever before in our history. Our people will not be found wanting. And attempts to change our status from Sovereign to serf will infuriate our people as nothing else will.

The oligarchy that now exists in Washington and New York and which has hijacked our Government has as its objective control of every facet of world trade and commerce and the installation of a world Government. The workers of the various countries around the world, including the United States are of no concern to these people. They are your most deadly enemy, and you must become aware of their penetration into our Government.

The President speaks often of "evildoers", referring to the people who attacked the World Trade Center. That may be, but the Sovereign American believes that a greater group of "evildoers" is right here at home in New York and Washington.

# CHAPTER 12

## REVOLUTION-IT WAS OUR GENESIS
## -IT WILL BE OUR REBIRTH!

Revolution! Are we afraid of that word? We should not be. We should glorify and revel in its meaning. It is how this country began. It is what our forefathers did to give us this grand land. Revolution is as natural to Americans as breathing. Breathing free. That is the key. Freedom. Revolution is a word we may become quite familiar with in the near future. It will be our salvation, freeing us from a federal Government that is becoming more and more unconstitutional every day.

Are we free now? Well, partially. Some freedom remains, but there are those who would enslave you economically, who would make you a serf in your own land, a part of a world Government, where you have no sovereignty, no right to fight back. They are in Washington and New York right now. They have made your own Government part of the cabal working against your continued freedom. And to take your sovereignty away from you.

But to Americans, sovereignty is everything. For each citizen is a sovereign in his own right. Your forefathers made you thus in 1776. And they gave you the 2nd Amendment to make sure you could always fight your own Government if necessary. To many Americans, that day is now approaching like a runaway freight train. So, do not fear revolution. Or secession. Secession is a form of revolution. Your forefathers made use of revolution many years ago. And southern forefathers made use of secession in 1861.

What are we to do? Are we to turn our backs while the ruthless oligarchy in Washington and New York completely destroys our form of Government? And delivers what is left to become subservient the United Nations?

Are we to let those who are looney liberals, faint-hearted, blame America first Americans, ride roughshod over us with the help of an overwhelmingly liberal press? Over the majority of patriotic Americans? All of this is happening, you know, in Washington and New York. It is happening in the media, in Hollywood, in the colleges and universities, where many, many individuals are selling a warped view of our traditions and history to our young. They are using a deliberate plan to denigrate anything in our history that enshrines our historic leaders and heroes alike.

Revolution or secession may be forced upon us by our own Government by unconstitutional efforts to enslave us under a world Government called the United Nations. That is what the Council on Foreign Relations would like. Not surprisingly, they are not asking your opinion on this matter.

But Governments never learn anything. The people cannot be suppressed, and efforts to do so will fail, especially here in America, where the Sons and Daughters of Liberty live. In case you don't recognize the name, the Sons of Liberty put on the Boston Tea Party, about the time this nation was born. It is part of your historical heritage. The Sovereign American cannot tell you to revolt against the Government, but it can tell you what your options are. You will have to decide what you do as a free, sovereign American. Whatever you decide, you cannot be stopped, no matter what you do. Your forefathers gave you the Declaration of Independence as your guide.

# CHAPTER 13

## THE NEW DECLARATION OF
## INDEPENDENCE OF 2002

When in the course of human events it becomes necessary for a People to dissolve the Political Bands which have connected them with a Government, and to assume among the Powers of the Earth, the separate and equal station to which the Laws of Nature and of Nature's God entitle them, a decent respect to the Opinions of Mankind requires that they should declare the causes which impel them to alter, change or dissolve their Government.

We hold these truths to be self-evident, that all men are created equal, that they are endowed by their creator with certain inalienable Rights, that among these are Life, Liberty, Privacy and the Pursuit of Happiness-That to secure these Rights, Governments are instituted among men, deriving their just Powers from the Consent of the Governed, that whenever any Form of Government becomes destructive of these Ends, it is the Right of the People to alter or abolish it, and to institute new Government, laying its Foundation on such Principles, and organizing its Powers in such Form, as to them shall seem most likely to effect their Safety and Happiness. Prudence indeed, will dictate that Governments long established should not be changed for light and transient Causes; and accordingly all Experience hath shown, that Mankind are more disposed to suffer, while Evils are sufferable, than to right themselves by abolishing the Forms to which they are accustomed. But when a long Train of Abuses and Usurpations, pursuing invariably the same Object, evinces a Design to reduce them under absolute Despotism, it is their Right, it is their Duty, to throw off such Government, and to provide new guards for their future security. Such has been the patient Sufferance of the various States of the Union, and their peoples, and such is now the Necessity which constrains them to alter their former Systems of Government. The History of the Government of the United States is a History of repeated Injuries and

Usurpations, all having as a direct Object the Establishment of an absolute Tyranny over the States and their People. To prove this, let facts be submitted to a candid World:

The Government of the United States has, in violation of the Constitution, introduced an Alien Organization, The United Nations, into the Political life of Americans, an Organization composed of Foreign Bureaucrats and Toadies whose Fealty lies with their own Governments, and not with that of the United States. This treachery was instituted during a time of war when 13 million American men were fighting World War II, and their attention was diverted away from the stealthy, subversive activities of their own Government.

The Government of the United States has wasted billions of dollars in taxes to support The United Nations and continues to do so, impoverishing its own citizens in the process in Violation of the Constitution.

The Government of the United States, in violation of the Constitution, supports the aims and objectives of the United Nations, which are to establish a World Government superior to that of the United States, which itself is unconstitutional, and further, conflicts with the good order and future well-being of the people of the United States.

The United States Government has consistently refused to submit the question of support for the United Nations to a National referendum so that the American People might repudiate it.

The United States Government in violation of the Constitution, has for more than fifty years, through Foreign Aid, wasted Billions of tax dollars to support alien nations, without the consent of the people.

The United States Government, in violation of the Constitution, has supported many Alien States of poor reputation to the detriment of their people and the people of the United States.

The United States Government, in violation of the Constitution, and at the Direction of the Council on Foreign Relations (CFR), a private, secret organization of elitists, has pursued an interventionist Foreign Policy, for the purpose of controlling trade around the World, to the detriment of the people of the United States.

The United States Government, in violation of the Constitution, and at the Direction of the Council on Foreign Relations, has pursued trade policies for more than fifty years that reduce jobs in America while transferring them to other countries, destroying and altering the lives of millions of Americans. This is the ultimate betrayal of the United States of its own citizens.

The United States Government, in violation of the Constitution, has allowed the Council on Foreign Relations, a secret, private organization to penetrate virtually every Department of the Government of the United States to control the Government and stifle the voice of the people and in the process destroy representative Government in the United States.

The United States Government, in violation of the Constitution, has allowed The Council on Foreign Relations, to usurp control over the Government that formerly rested with the people by means of their votes, through bribery and control of politicians.

The United States Government, in violation of the Constitution, has allowed Military leaders of the United States to become members of the Council on Foreign Relations, where they are continually propagandized in the aims and objectives of the CFR, a direct conflict with their oath to support the Constitution which they swore as Military officers.

The United States Government, through its control over Congress, in violation of the Constitution, established a privately owned Central Bank, which is vested with control over every aspect of the financial health of the United States, and operates to utilize its control over the American People which previously rested with the Congress. In abdicating its control over the economy of the United States, the Congress has been guilty of little less than treason.

The United States Government, in violation of the Constitution, in the pursuit of free trade, has eliminated tariffs on foreign imports, and transferred these costs to the American people.

The United States Government has instituted vast and onerous taxes designed to impoverish the people of the United States, in order to pursue the goals of the CFR and therefore, the United Nations.

The United States Government, in violation of the Constitution, has instituted a system of withholding taxes for every employed person in the nation, and that system takes their tax money from them before they ever receive it. This system places them into involuntary servitude to the Government, as surely as any slave was involuntarily locked to a slave owner. This is one of the most ruthless plans ever devised by any Government to enslave and control its own people.

The United States Government, through its spokesmen have spread lies about the Sovereignty of the United States, which is an attack on each American Citizen, since they are the only Sovereigns in the Nation.

The United States Government, in violation of the Constitution, through its policies of maintaining open borders, has permitted the various States, and the Nation, to be invaded by domestic enemies of the Constitution, millions of illegal and legal Aliens, to an extent that the future of the Republic is in grave danger of dissolution and destruction of its Union.

The United States Government has erected a multitude of new offices and Departments, and sent hither swarms of officers to establish rules and regulations that harass the People and eat out their substance.

The United States Government, in violation of the Constitution, has, through Executive Orders, sought to transfer military officers and men, to Alien Organizations, The United Nations and NATO.

The United States Government, in Violation of the Constitution, has sought to subordinate American Sovereignty to the control of the United Nations and various other International bodies such as the World Court and World Trade Organization.

The United States Government, in Violation of the Constitution, has waged war on the American People, at Ruby Ridge and Waco, and in acts of perfidy, killed men, women and children, and destroyed a Church not of their liking. These are the acts of a Tyrannical, Rogue Government, operating outside the norms expected of a civilized Nation. The Government took no action to punish those responsible for such savagery, but indeed, rewarded them with promotions and medals at a secret, unpublicized ceremony.

The United States Government by its unconstitutional actions, has excited domestic Insurrection among us at Oklahoma City, Oklahoma, Seattle, Washington, New York, New York and other locales, violating Domestic Tranquility and good order. The Government has incited War against the United States by Foreign States and their peoples, who are opposed to the policies of the Government which pursue control of International trade and which serve International organizations and not the peoples of those lands, or the United States. This resulted in the attack against the World Trade Center in New York City in September of 2001.

The United States Government, in violation of the Declaration of Independence and the Constitution, has established a superior class of Citizen in the United States, by protecting them against all manner of anticipated activities on the part of the people, whom they have identified as terrorists if they take action. These "special Citizens" are called Federal Employees, from the lowest clerk to the highest politicians and ex-politicians.

The United States Government, in violation of the Constitution, has militarized local police units by training them in military tactics at Government facilities.

The United States Government, in violation of the Constitution, has caused Military units of the United States to practice suppression of the people by initiating military exercises among our villages, towns and cities, without the permission of the local authorities, and have conducted similar exercises using military helicopters to invade villages and towns in the dead of night, causing great confusion, consternation and suspicion among our citizens.

The United States Government, in violation of the Constitution, has caused the Military of the United States to, in combination with foreign military forces, practice invasions of the United States without informing the people of the true nature of such exercises, causing great suspicion among our citizens.

The United States Government, in violation of the Constitution, has surveyed military units to inquire whether soldiers of those units would fire upon Americans citizens who, having been ordered to give up their weapons (a violation of the 2nd Amendment of the Constitution), refused such an order.

The United States Government, in Violation of the Constitution, has repeatedly waged war against sovereign foreign States and their peoples without a Declaration of War from the Congress, as required by the Constitution.

The United States Government, in violation of the Constitution, waged an undeclared war in Viet Nam for more than ten years, a war in which the armed forces of the United States were not permitted to win and during which more than 50,000 young Americans were killed. A war which incited riots and great unrest within our populace and forced some Americans to flee to Canada for refuge. It is the most shameful example of Governmental misuse of its powers in the history of the United States, a period that will live in infamy. Yet no politician, no leader of any civilian rank ever was prosecuted or charged with any crime against the people. A travesty of Government at it's worst.

The United States Government, in violation of the Constitution, seeks a state of perpetual war against sovereign foreign States, behind which furtherance of the aims of the Council on Foreign Relations and the United Nations can be extended.

The United States Government, in violation of the Constitution, has established Federal Police Forces to control the people, and allowed them to identify themselves as police officers. There is no provision in the Constitution to allow establishment of a Federal Police Force.

The United States Government, in violation of the Constitution, has for more than half a century blackmailed the several states into submission, requiring them to comply with federal programs and legislation they would otherwise oppose, on pain of loss of federal dollars otherwise due the states.

In every stage of these oppressions and usurpations the People of the United States have expressed their dismay and Petitioned for Redress in the most humble terms to the Government, through their elected Representatives in Congress, to no avail. Their repeated Petitions have been answered only by repeated Injury. The Government has been deaf to the voice of Justice and of consanguinity, and as a result less than half of the People vote in national elections, and great suspicion of Government and politicians exists across the country.

We therefore, the Sovereign Citizens of the United States of America, in electronic Congress assembled, appealing to the Supreme Judge of the World for the Rectitude of our Intentions, do, in the name, and by the authority of the good Citizens of this Country, solemnly Publish and Declare that these United States, free, Sovereign and independent, and having observed that the Government has lost the consent of the people, further declare that the former Government is null and void and dissolved. It is further declared that all laws passed by the Congress since January 1, 1900, that include unconstitutional provisions or sections, are null, void and without effect, It is declared also that as free and independent people and States, they have full power to establish a new Government, levy war, conclude peace, contract alliances, establish commerce and do all other acts and things which independent States may of right do. And for the support of this Declaration, with a reliance on the protection of divine providence, we mutually pledge to each other our lives, our fortunes, and our sacred honor.

# CHAPTER 14

## THE WORDS OF OUR GREATEST PRESIDENT

Modern politics in the United States has produced a flow of small men into the Presidency. We do not have statesmen, we have politicians, most of whom wouldn't recognize a statesman if they were fortunate enough to meet one. Some were even downright lowlifes. Clinton was one of these. Ford fell out of every doorway he encountered. Nixon had traits of greatness but was terribly flawed. Bush, the elder, served dark masters, as did Clinton, Carter and others before them. Franklin Roosevelt was a traitor who led us into war while proclaiming the opposite. Truman was a patriot who could not be led astray by those around him who tried and failed in that enterprise. He was the last populist President.

Throughout this publication, you have noticed that the Sovereignty of the American people has been proclaimed in absolute terms. Aside from the Declaration of Independence, which made us Sovereigns, and the Constitution, which made us armed Sovereigns, only one President ever uttered words which confirmed those facts. But one did, and he was our greatest President and a statesman of renown. Every American should review the words he spoke during a time of crisis in our Nation, the possible breakup of the Union as the Civil War approached. He was Abraham Lincoln. At his first inaugural, his address contained the following words:

"This country, with its institutions, belongs to the people who inhabit it. Whenever they shall grow weary of the existing Government, they can exercise their Constitutional right of amending it, or their revolutionary right to dismember it or overthrow it."

"While I make no recommendation of amendments, I fully recognize the rightful authority of the people over the whole subject, to be exercised in either of the modes prescribed in the instrument itself;..."

He said further: "The chief magistrate derives all his authority from the people, and they have conferred none upon him to fix terms for the separation of the states. The people themselves can do this also if they choose; but the executive, as such, has nothing to do with it. His duty is to administer the present Government as it came to his hands, and to transmit it, unimpaired, by him, to his successor."

Is it any wonder why the Sovereign American venerates this remarkable statesman? Why we refer to him as our greatest President? Measure our Presidents from Wilson forward, and make your own assessment. We have no statesmen today, only small characters in an office that cries out for greatness. The American people deserve no less.

# CHAPTER 15

## WHO ARE THE MEMBERS OF THE COUNCIL ON FOREIGN RELATIONS?

The total membership of the CFR now stands at about 3900 individuals. Using the CFR's own data, the profile of the membership is as follows:

| Location | No. of Members | % of Membership |
|---|---|---|
| New York area | 1283 | 32 |
| Washington, D.C. | 1253 | 32 |
| National (includes overseas) | 1452 | 36 |
| **Total** | **3988** | **100** |
| | | |
| **Profession:** | **No. of Members** | **% of Membership** |
| Business | 1240 | 31 |
| Professors, Fellows& Researchers | 731 | 18 |
| Nonprofit | 600 | 15 |
| Government Officials | 503 | 13 |
| Lawyers | 332 | 8 |
| University & College Administrators | 279 | 7 |
| Journalists, correspondents & Editors | 240 | 6 |
| Other | 63 | 2 |
| Total | 3988 | 100 |

It is of considerable interest that the preponderance of members are in business. It is also of great interest that 503 members are in Government. The next most interesting number is that of the Professors, Fellows and Researchers. When University and College Administrators are added in, a total of 1010 Academicians are members, or 25 % of the total.

Why should this be the case? The answer is that there has always been a strong connection between the CFR and these people, because many members rotate between Government and various Universities where their employment enables them to continue research and propaganda. This situation operates like a revolving door, but it would not be possible without the cooperation of the people who run the institutions, the Administrators. Collusion is another word for their actions.

The final number of interest is that of Journalists, Correspondents and Editors. Why would such people become members of an organization that forbids its members to reveal what transpires in their meetings? Why would they condone censorship, the very thought of which sends most newsmen into fits of outrage? The answer is that they are of the same mind as the leadership of the CFR. As members, they are used as propagandists for the organization. Do you really think you can trust what you hear on the evening news? Oh, didn't you know? At least two network anchors are members. Isn't that interesting. So are many of the talking heads you see on TV every weekend. Where in the news media are the rest of the 240 members? You would have to examine the membership list to find out. But the Sovereign American knows where they are.

One must always remember that the CFR selects its members. They are invited to join. You are not. They want only people they can use. And control.

# CHAPTER 16

## DOMESTIC ENEMIES

When the Vice President of the United States and all members of the military take their oaths of office or enlistment, they are required to swear to Defend the Constitution of the United States against all enemies, foreign and domestic. (The president, curiously, merely swears to preserve, protect and defend the Constitution. Nothing in his oath refers to domestic enemies. Why is that?)

Who are the domestic enemies? They are enemies of the Constitution. They are not identified in the Founding Documents, but the Declaration of Independence gives the people of the United States wide powers to, at any time, declare an existing Government to be null and void, and to replace it with a new Government of their choosing. It therefore follows that if the entire Government may be repudiated by the people, the people may also identify those enemies of the Constitution that may exist at any given time.

The powers of the people are those of a Sovereign. There is no greater power in the United States. The uniqueness of the Declaration of Independence lies in the fact that it delegates to the people complete power over everything in the land. There is no higher power; not the President, not the Congress, not the Supreme Court, not any branch of Government or individual of the Government. The Founding fathers made each citizen of the United States a Sovereign in his own right.

Who are the domestic enemies of the Constitution? They may be identified by several categories of people. International Bankers. Free-traders. Globalists. Some newsmen, broadcasters, and anyone associated with, or who supports, the United Nations. Those whose activities are aligned with the organizations and Corporations operating in concert with those mentioned. Every member of the Council on Foreign Relations is a Domestic Enemy because that organization supports the creation of a UN world

Government superior to the United States. Every American member of the Trilateral Commission, the sister organization of the CFR, is a domestic enemy.

CFR members exist in all levels of Government, media and business, placed there by executives beholden to the directors of globalism and their cohorts. Most such Government employees are non- elected appointees, installed in office by those who were elected.

But there is an even greater danger to the Republic from domestic enemies in the massive numbers of illegal aliens who have been permitted to invade our country by several successive administrations. These people do not belong here, but because they are here, they are domestic enemies.

Those who are here legally but who will not assimilate into our society also are domestic enemies. They seek to eventually control the Republic. In that moment, America will cease to be an independent nation and will become something else. The entire question of legal and illegal immigration is one of the greatest betrayals by a Government of its people in history. By its unconstitutional handling of immigration, the Government has betrayed Americans in a most fundamental way.

Illegal and legal immigration is the method by which some enemies of the Constitution intend to change the United States in unconstitutional ways, and to eventually establish foreign control over everything in the United States. Americans will have to combat this wave of change in basic, forceful ways, and even eventually, secession or revolution, if it is not stopped while it can still be stopped without bloodshed.

# CHAPTER 17

## GLOBALISM AND YOU

Globalism is the modern version of the ancient European system of controlling people called Feudalism. The system included manors-land holdings of the enlightened- which were in the hands of a Lord. The Lord in turn reigned over serfs and villeins, slaves if you will. There is no difference in the modern version, although slaves are not so identified, but the workers of the world are no less slaves than their ancient brothers. Nothing has changed, except that the United States is now the author of the new system. Globalism is a totally manufactured system, created by the Council on Foreign Relations and the Trilateral Commission, and is intended to benefit international banks, Wall Street and International corporations. The ruthless, rich and powerful still control the poor and powerless. And if they have their way, they always will. And now they control the United States Government.

The CFR and the Trilateral Commission (TC), have their headquarters in New York and Washington. These are secretive and powerful organizations run by a single-minded aristocracy which is determined to control the economy of the world. And they are succeeding because the average person has no idea about what they're up to.

If you think, as Americans, that you are somehow protected from globalism, you are sadly mistaken. The reason labor rates are so low in the United States is that Corporations, who support the CFR, want low labor rates. They would pay you nothing if they could get away with it. Labor Unions are of no help-the reason? Their leaders are members of the CFR. Your Congressman or Senator, who may be a member of the CFR, is of no help, because he or she, long ago, bought into globalism as a philosophy. They are part of the problem.

Always remember. The propaganda that tells you every day that globalism and free trade are good for you and the United States is a lie. Globalism and free trade are good only for large Corporations, most of them international in size. And any Corporation would enslave you in a minute if they could. They are already well along on that path and will continue to the end if we do not stop them.

Your Government will not lift a hand to do it-the Government has been hijacked by the CFR. And the great Corporations go right on with their plans, even including the illegal acts that have recently come to light about how CEO's, accountants and stock analysts have cheated not only stockholders but the general public. Billions of dollars are involved in this thievery.

All around the world people are rioting to stop globalism at every meeting of Government leaders (the G-8) but those Governments, including the United States, stop the people by use of steel fencing and massive forces of police and troops.

In the United States, this whole scenario is unconstitutional. The Government cannot incite the people to riot for any reason. The globalist policies they pursue are unconstitutional because of the affect they have on the people and their jobs. The Government is terrified of you, but they press on just the same because you are not organized. That is why you must protect your rights. The second Amendment is all that stands between you and the serfs of Europe and Africa.

If there were no second Amendment, how many years ago would you have been enslaved? Five years? Twenty years? A century? At least that many. Probably more.

The rioters around the world have not yet realized that they are fighting in the wrong arena. Once they understand that the headquarters of globalism are in New York and Washington, they can make more direct attacks against the head of the snake. Fighting the snake at its tail is not effective. The matters the G-8 discusses at their meetings around the world are already settled, in New York and Washington. They are merely talking about how to implement the latest decisions of their leaders. They are the tail of the snake. Much to our shame, the head of the snake lies in its lofty towers of New York and Washington, where it is secure from Government action. It owns the Government.

# CHAPTER 18

## THE PRESIDENCY

While the President of the United States is often an admirable person, the Chief Executive over time has viewed his office in far more expansive terms than either the Founding Fathers or the populace at large.

The President nowadays is far more interested in Foreign Affairs than many Americans think he should be. In fact, it is the opinion of the Sovereign American that the President now believes himself to be President of the World. Presidents no longer seem able to stay at home, flitting here and there to meet with G-8 leaders (the infamous group of leaders concerned with international trade and finance matters), giving away your hard earned tax dollars and demanding special trade authority from the Congress.

Presidents are now enamored of Executive Orders, illegal and unconstitutional orders that the President issues on his own to achieve an end. There is no authority in the Constitution for such orders, but the Congress does not challenge him when they are issued. Thus not only the President is operating outside the Constitution, but the Congress is abetting his actions.

The Sovereign American further believes that the President of the United States should not be conspiring with other Governments to control trade for the benefit of the Council on Foreign Relations and the Trilateral Commission, both of which are private organizations controlled by a wealthy oligarchy. The euphemism of "Free Trade" is often used as an excuse to take such actions, but the premise is false. There is no such thing as free trade, it has never existed in any country. But American Presidents and the wealthy oligarchy in Washington seek to control all trade in the world, and such falsehoods are their methodology of choice.

And in recent years Americans have come to realize that there is a great need for much closer observation of candidates for the highest office in the land. Experience has shown that unsavory characters are attempting to land the position so enamoring to politicians. This country has no desire or need to place a degenerate into the Presidency. But recent experience has been a great teacher. Again, eternal vigilance is required.

Since WW II the office of the President has been occupied by members of the Council on Foreign Relations(CFR) or the Trilateral Commission (TC), or both. (Although there is no evidence that the current President is a member of either organization, one can be sure that former President Bush still talks to his son. The former President was a member of both the CFR and the Trilateral Commission.) It is no wonder that the Government of the United States is now shot through with members of the CFR in virtually every department of the Government, including the Supreme Court. It is no wonder that the CFR controls everything the Government does. Including the actions of the President.

# CHAPTER 19

## THE DANGERS OF GRADUALISM
## AND THE FUTURE

It is one of the truths about any population, (and Americans are no different than the peoples of any other country), is that changes made over a period of years are much more likely to succeed than changes made abruptly. The people of the Council On Foreign Relations (CFR) know this very well, and it has been a hallmark of their activities for fifty years.

No one in the late 1940's and early 1950's realized what was being done to the country and the people by stealth, largely during WW II. The beginning penetration of the Government by the disciples of stealth. The establishment of the United Nations Charter. The conferences at Bretton Woods that changed monetary systems worldwide and legislation that spawned the World Bank and the International Money Fund.

But the greatest travesty ever foisted on the American people was the withholding tax. This nefarious plan, devised by a bureaucrat in the Roosevelt Administration, ensured for all time that the American people could not mount a tax revolt against the Government. It locked the American people into involuntary servitude to the Government. That involuntary servitude still chains every American to a Government we no longer control through our votes.

Moneyed interests, banks and Corporations now control our Government and have, since those days so long ago. More and more our people are locked in a financial box, with only the smallest minority able to amass much money. The great bulk of the people are trapped, strapped by ever rising costs, and ever more foreign products that they are forced by reduced circumstances to buy. By now many Americans realize that their own Government wants them to be servile and unable to resist a further decline in their purchasing power or the continuing push for more free trade and more immigrants to feed the corporations of the country.

What can the people do? Short of secession or revolution, nothing. But we are fast approaching the same situation our forefathers faced in the 1700's. Only this time it's not King George, it's the despotic state of our own Government that we must oppose, and God willing, change forever. For if we do not, our children and grandchildren will have to do it for us, and they may lose their lives in the doing of it. Or live in a deeper servile status into a very dark future.

We cannot leave it for our posterity to reclaim our Government. We must do it while there is still time to do it. We might get hurt, in many ways, but it will be nothing compared to what will take place if we delay the day of reckoning.

# CHAPTER 20

## THE COST OF CHANGING GOVERNMENTS

No American who understands the functioning of the Corporations and the wealthy and powerful men who have hijacked our Government, has any illusions about how they will react to anyone who proposes change in Government. And how they will react when changes come, as they surely will.

They will resist any change that adversely affects their interests, and their reaction will be powerful and ruthless. One can expect rejected politicians and bureaucrats to seek retribution, and they will move heaven and earth to immediately create a new war, recession, or depression, with the objective being the destabilization of the new Government, and to impoverish the people; to bring them to their knees economically. They will work to create strife and division among the people, during which they will try to regain power. Already several such factors are a reality. The President seeks to lead us into a new war with Iraq, with little justification. Already the vast surpluses which only a few months ago stretched as far into the future as one could see, have not only vanished, but have been replaced by new deficits. The plain truth of the matter is that our huge Government is no longer trustworthy, and has not been since WW II. We must change it, as is our right under the founding documents of this country.

There will be a period of adjustment when any new Government takes over. There will be people forced out of their jobs in Government, and hopefully, out of Washington. They will not go quietly or gracefully. They will seek to demean the new Government, to bring pressure to bear on anyone responsible for the change. And they will be aided and abetted by the national media. It will require determination and patience on the part of the new administration and the people.

The new Government may be forced to destroy many Government buildings lest they be reoccupied by faceless bureaucrats. Congress must be restrained in its role as financiers of the Government. No new appropriations for rejected programs or facilities can be tolerated. And the long- lived pork programs the Congress is so fond of must be eliminated completely. The new Government must control expenditures with a firm hand. Yet the fight will have to be conducted within the Constitution. There can be no attempt to deny free speech or interfere with the press or to eliminate any person's rights, although rejected politicians and bureaucrats must not be permitted in the new Government. The wealthy individuals who have hijacked our Government must be prosecuted and sentenced to long prison terms for their transgressions.

Changing the Government is not accomplished every day. It will be difficult and will consume many days, even several years. But in the end, the people will be freer than they have been in a century. It is their destiny continuing into the future.

# CHAPTER 21

## THE CONSTITUTION OF THE UNITED STATES

Our forefathers considered long and hard the Government they wanted to survive in the new world. No one can read the Constitution and the Federalist Papers without realizing the effort that went into the creation of this new kind of Government. They wanted a Republic-yes, the one you used to swear allegiance to in school, and it's shining flag that has led so many of us in difficult times.

The Constitution and its Bill Of Rights, is a living document, a document for all ages. But there is a problem today that our forefathers did not foresee. That problem is about a Supreme Court that after more than two hundred years, interprets the Constitution as it sees fit, often to achieve an end. But that is a correctable problem. There is a more pressing problem. That is that there is already talk of suspending the Constitution in time of war or a "declared emergency."

There is no provision in the Constitution to provide for an interregnum of it's effectiveness. The Constitution cannot be suspended except by an unconstitutional act on the part of the Government or any politician who would attempt the act. No one who is a part of the three branches of the Government can legally try to stop the effect of the Constitution, under any circumstances, war or peace, civil strife, invasion, pestilence or earthquake. It cannot be done.

Yet there are those Americans, largely newsmen, who incredibly, call for this very act. It is a matter of treason, and should be cause for prosecution.

For Americans, after the Declaration of Independence, there is no greater or significant document in the world than the Constitution of the United States. Its protections are those every American depends upon. The Bill of Rights, so much under attack in the last decade, are the lifeblood of Americans, and no one must be permitted to change or eliminate them, no matter whether they are

Domestic Enemies or foreign born. The Sovereign American is dedicated to exposing all who would do so.

But changes are needed in the Constitution. Our forefathers never dreamed that an oligarchy would rise in this country and become powerful enough to take over the Government. Yet that is what has happened. Since WW II, the Council on Foreign Relations (a private organization) has penetrated our Government and sent its members to run for high office innumerable times, so that even more members might be placed in the various departments of the Government. Were our forefathers alive today, all the members of this organization would be executed. Unfortunately they are not alive, and we are stuck with an ersatz Government, unelected and out of control. A new Government of the people must take office and the activities of the CFR and other like organizations must be made unconstitutional. This must be handled by a Constitutional Amendment.

In fact many changes must be made in the Constitution. But to learn about such changes the reader must first read Chapter 13 before proceeding to Chapter 22.

# CHAPTER 22

## PROPOSED CHANGES IN THE CONSTITUTION

It has already been stated in this publication, that if the people are successful in ousting the previous Government, there would be no immediate need to rewrite the Constitution to make changes that are necessary; a new Congress and determined President could make the necessary changes in law to protect the new Government and the people. But if the people, in their judgment, feel that a new Constitutional Convention must be called, as is their right, the following Amendments must be considered. But all should be alert to the interference of the old Government and its adherents and supporters, who will do anything to disrupt and change the good intentions of the new Convention. WARNING! WARNING! No person who supports the old Government and its objectives must be permitted to take part in the new Constitutional Convention.

After two hundred twenty six years, it is apparent that changes must be made in the basic law of the land if the land is not to be balkanized by various pressure groups. Should political and philosophical balkanization take place, the Union cannot long survive. Such balkanization will surely lead to the fate of most lands where democracy flourished for a period of years, but eventually succumbed to factional pressures. All Americans must remember that we live in a Constitutional Republic, where the most good for the most people is achieved by hewing to middle ground. As always in America, while minority views must be allowed to flourish, there is no substitute for majority rule.

Delegates to the Constitutional Convention shall be chosen by the people of the various states, and shall require no qualifications other than that they must be citizens of the United States and the State which they shall represent, and be at least 50 years of age. Delegates must reflect the makeup of the population of citizens nationally, by applicable percentage. The presence of illegal aliens or any foreigners ineligible to vote, in any state or the nation at large shall be ignored when allotting percentages to the delegates. No court, including the Supreme Court shall hear any case challenging this Amendment.

No law shall be written by the Congress or any State Legislature that extends the rights of American citizens to illegal aliens or foreigners visiting or working in this country. The Supreme Court and all inferior courts shall not hear cases challenging any aspect of this Amendment.

No law shall be written, nor shall the Supreme Court hear cases where individual behavior is involved. Human behavior, with all its faults is God-given, and neither man nor court, shall attempt to change or eliminate that which is contained in our bodies, minds and souls. Man's freedom is absolute. That being true, the whole man is free. So-called hate crimes especially are crimes prosecutable under other laws, and no type of add-on law attacking human behavior shall be permitted. No court, including the Supreme Court, shall hear any case challenging this Amendment.

The right of privacy of individuals is absolute, and shall not be contravened by any individual, organization, or court. No court, including the Supreme Court, shall hear any case challenging this Amendment.

No person or organization, including religious, shall intimidate another person by confrontation, word of mouth or visual depiction of a supposed status or because of a contemplated course of action. The right of individual privacy is absolute. No court, including the Supreme Court, shall hear any case challenging this Amendment.

No person or organization may seek to change laws or regulations except in relation to the number of believers as compared to the whole of society. Less than 15 percent of the total population shall be cause for rejection. No court, including the Supreme Court shall hear any case challenging this Amendment.

No private organization may seek to advise or involve itself in the operation of Government, and members of Government organizations shall not belong to such organizations. No person shall be elected or appointed to any office of Government who is or has been a member of such organizations. No court, including the Supreme Court, shall hear any case challenging this Amendment.

The President of the United States or any other person or organization may not persuade, require or induce the Congress of the United States to eliminate or alter its responsibilities under the Constitution. No legislation may be completed and become law until the Congress approves it in all its parts and is subjected to the amendment process. Legislation to the contrary shall not become law. Violation of this Amendment shall be cause for impeachment of the President and loss of citizenship. No court, including the Supreme Court, shall hear any case challenging this Amendment.

No law shall be written or altered by any person other than a Representative elected for that purpose. No Representative shall delegate that task to another. To do so shall make the Representative unqualified to sit in Congress. Violation of this Amendment shall be punishable by a fine of 500,000 dollars and imprisonment of twenty five years. No court, including the Supreme Court shall hear any case challenging this Amendment.

The President of the United States shall not travel to foreign lands for the purpose of arranging trade agreements. All such contacts with foreign lands and their leaders shall be conducted by the appropriate office of each State, with the advice of the Congress. No subsequent trade agreement shall become law until approved by the States and Congress. A two thirds vote is required for approval. No court, including the Supreme Court shall hear any case challenging this Amendment.

The President of the United States when traveling abroad or at any other time, shall not dispense funds or other assets, including military, of the United States to foreign leaders, states or organizations. No court including the Supreme Court shall hear any case challenging this Amendment.

No trade agreement with foreign Governments or lands shall become law if the agreement results in loss of American employment or the movement of such employment to foreign locations. No court, including the Supreme Court shall hear any case challenging this Amendment.

No trade agreement or movement of goods to foreign lands shall become law or in effect until approved by the Defense department. No court, including the Supreme Court shall hear any case challenging this Amendment.

American or foreign-owned businesses may not move to foreign lands in search of lower wage levels or other advantages unless a penalty equal to the net worth of the company is paid to the State where the company is located. American and foreign owned businesses moving overseas shall be required to pay a 1000% import duty on products manufactured or produced in such facilities if brought to the United States, in any manner, for sale. No court, including the Supreme Court, shall hear any case challenging this Amendment.

Foreign countries may provide access to the American market for their domestic companies by paying an annual access fee of the United States Treasury in advance. The fee shall be adjusted as required but in no case shall be less than the total expected dollar value of the trade annually as determined by the Commerce Department. No foreign-owned business may operate in the United States unless Americans own 51 percent of the company stock. No court, including the Supreme Court, shall hear any case challenging this Amendment.

The Supreme Court shall not create new law, that being the province of the Congress. The judgments of the Court shall be based only on the original wording of the Constitution or its succeeding document. Changes to the wording of the Constitution, or of the meaning of its wording, shall render subsequent decisions of the Court null and void, and shall be sufficient cause for dismissal of the members of the Court involved. No court, including the

Supreme Court, shall hear any case challenging this Amendment.

No Court, including the Supreme Court shall render opinions that nullify or overturn referendums, initiatives or other votes of the people, or cause taxes to be imposed or raised. Laws generated by Court fiat shall be unconstitutional. No court, including the Supreme Court, shall hear any case challenging this Amendment.

No member of any court, including the Supreme Court, shall continue in office except by sufferance of the people. Regular elections, at ten year intervals are required for continued service. No court, including the Supreme Court, shall hear any case challenging this Amendment.

A negative referendum or vote of the people, even if initiated by the people, shall constitute reason for immediate dismissal of members of any court. No court, including the Supreme Court, shall hear any case challenging this Amendment.

No member of Congress shall vote in opposition to the will of the people of his district. No member of Congress shall vote his personal feelings or inclination, but shall only vote the will of his constituents. A vote to the contrary shall be cause for ejection from the Congress, and cause for disqualification for any office of the Government at any level in the several states. No court, including the Supreme Court, shall hear any case challenging this Amendment.

The Supreme Court shall sit in six months of the year, but shall be required to work at least 12 months of each year or 2000 hours per year or the same number of hours as the average citizen, and shall take no more than two weeks vacation annually. The Court shall hear no more than six cases per year, and issue no more than six judgments per year. No court, including the Supreme Court, shall hear any case challenging this Amendment.

The Congress shall meet at least once annually in the Capitol in Washington, D.C. All Congressmen and Senators shall maintain and work from their office in their home district, where they shall be available for consultation with

US citizens. All members of both houses shall maintain encrypted electronic contact with their fellow members as required via secure lines. If their presence in Washington is required by special circumstances, they shall temporarily reside in a hotel acquired and operated by the federal Government for that purpose. Except in time of war or national emergency, both houses of Congress shall pass no more than six laws per year. No law passed by the Congress shall adversely affect any citizen of the US. No court, including the Supreme Court shall hear any case challenging this Amendment, or the Amendment itself.

Organized, paid lobbying by any organization, company or group shall be a felony. No organization, company, group, or party, except individual private Citizens of the United States shall contact any Congressman or Senator. No lobbyist for any organization or group shall give money or anything of value, including services, to any Congressman or Senator at any time. Violations of this Amendment shall result in imprisonment of perpetrator and Congressman or Senator of not less than twenty years and a fine of not less than a million dollars. No court, including the Supreme Court shall hear any case challenging this Amendment.

No court, including the Supreme Court, shall hear any case involving the freedoms of the American people, nor shall it render any decisions that affect or negate such freedoms. The freedoms of the American people are absolute and shall not be infringed upon or altered by any court. No court, including the Supreme Court, shall hear any case challenging this Amendment.

No court, including the Supreme Court shall hear any case involving the rights of the American people. The rights of the American people are absolute and shall not be abridged in any manner by any court. No court, including the Supreme Court, shall hear any case challenging this Amendment.

No court shall hear any case brought by a Corporation whose net worth is more than 20,000,000 dollars or other like organization, against an individual American citizen. No court, including the Supreme Court, shall hear any case challenging this Amendment.

No court shall issue a search warrant permitting the seizure of private property, including firearms of any type, computers or parts thereof, or personal papers of any American citizen. Seizure of such materials violate the Second, Fourth and Fifth Amendments to the Constitution, and its provisions against self-incrimination. No court, including the Supreme Court shall hear any case challenging this Amendment.

The wording of the 2nd Amendment of the Constitution shall be changed as follows." An armed populace being essential to the Republic, the right of American citizens to keep and bear arms of any sort shall not be infringed." No court, including the Supreme Court shall hear any case challenging this Amendment.

No Congressman or Senator may change his party affiliation except at the end of his term. If elected, as a Republican or Democrat, or any other party, to change parties within the term of his election, the election would be nullified and the people disenfranchised, which is unconstitutional. Once elected, the Representative or Senator must serve out his term without change. No court, including the Supreme Court, shall hear any case challenging this Amendment.

Congress shall make no law appropriating funds from the Treasury for the purpose of supporting any foreign Government in any manner. No court, including the Supreme Court, shall hear any case challenging this Amendment.

The Congress shall make no appropriations in support of the United Nations or any of its subordinate organizations, including the International Money Fund and the World Bank. No court, including the Supreme Court shall hear any case challenging this Amendment.

No corporation may negotiate or deal with foreign countries at any level in the course of conducting their business affairs. All such negotiations shall be the function of the State in which the Corporation resides, and the State and Defense Departments with the advice of the Commerce Department, under the supervision of the Congress. No court, including the Supreme Court, shall hear any case challenging this Amendment.

The rights of the States shall be absolute, and superior to those of the Federal Government in all respects except national defense, air traffic control, the Postal Service and the Social security System. No court, including the Supreme Court shall hear any case challenging this Amendment.

Except for the District of Columbia, the federal Government shall hold title to no lands. All other federal lands shall be owned, operated and supervised by the state in which it is located. Federal title to such lands shall be transferred to the applicable State without delay. Operation by the state shall function to give the greatest possible access to the American people for their recreation, or to foreign visitors, yet consistent with the needs of the inhabitants of the State. The federal Government shall have no part in the operation, management or supervision of such lands. The federal Government shall reduce its budget by the amount of the funds previously budgeted for federal lands, and discharge federal employees previously employed for the purpose. No court, including the Supreme Court, shall hear any case challenging any part of this Amendment.

All Federal taxes levied on and approved by the people, shall become due and payable on the 1st of April each year, but shall be submitted to the State, which shall deduct moneys owed to the State by the Federal Government, so long as the State shall not be in contest with the Federal Government in any case at law. The State shall assure its superiority to the federal Government before submitting tax money to the national Government. No court, including the Supreme Court, shall hear any case challenging this Amendment.

The Federal Government shall not install any taxation plan that takes tax money from individuals in any State before the individual receives it. The taxation plan known as a "withholding" plan shall be specifically eliminated. No court, including the Supreme Court shall hear any case challenging this Amendment or reinstituting such a plan in the United States.

The federal Government shall not interfere with the activities or policies of the several States, each state and its citizens being sovereign in both respects. The rights of the people are superior to that of the States in which they reside. No court, including the Supreme Court, shall hear any case challenging this Amendment.

All rights are reserved for the people in all states and the nation. No Government, Federal, state or local, shall extend privileges to the people, in any form. Any privileges created by the States or national Government are in reality rights of the people, and the people shall automatically own them, and use them for their own purposes. No court, including the Supreme Court shall hear cases to the contrary.

At no level of Government shall any fees be attached to the rights of the people. No court, including the Supreme Court shall rule otherwise.

No court, including the Supreme Court shall hear any case challenging the rights of the people in any respect. No court shall hear any case challenging the right of the people to throw off their Government at any time, and to supplant such Government with a new Government more to their liking. No court, including the Supreme Court, shall hear any case challenging this Amendment.

The congress shall write no law concerning labor rights, and shall not interfere with labor negotiations in any manner. The Taft-Hartley law is specifically ruled null and void. No court, including the Supreme Court, shall hear any case challenging this Amendment.

Congress shall write laws that limit the power of international corporations and banks to operate within and without the United States. Such laws shall set financial limits on the size of corporations at not more than 100 million dollars. International banks shall be banned within the

United States. All banks shall conduct 100% of their business within the United States and with US citizens and businesses owned by Americans. All banks shall be limited in their ability to transfer funds overseas for any purpose, and shall not do so without the approval of Congress. Yearly audits of such movements shall be required. No court, including the Supreme Court, shall hear any case challenging these laws or this Amendment.

Corporations and banks shall be required to limit their size, and shall not acquire other Corporations, banks or subsidiaries without the approval of Congress. Previously acquired corporations, etc., shall be divested at once. Both horizontal and vertical growth shall be limited as the people require. Banks shall not become a growth based industry but shall serve only the American people and businesses. No court, including the Supreme Court, shall hear any case challenging this Amendment.

Government shall not institute the use of a central bank, and all monetary policy shall be conducted and administered by the Congress in accordance with the Constitution. A Federal Reserve system is specifically prohibited and void in the United States. The money issued by the Federal Reserve in the previous Government, being worthless, shall be replaced within five years of the new Government taking office. No court, including the Supreme Court, shall hear any case challenging this Amendment.

The right of an American citizen to make a citizen's arrest, shall be upheld by all courts and law enforcement organizations in the United States. No court, including the Supreme Court, shall hear any suit brought challenging such rights.

The right of American citizens to close the borders of the United States, or any roadway, seaport or airport providing access to the Nation, for any reason, shall be inviolate, and shall be upheld by all courts, including the Supreme Court. No court, including the Supreme Court, shall hear cases brought to repeal, alter or challenge this right.

The right of American citizens to assemble freely shall not be abridged. No Government agency or department, shall place any gathering of citizens under surveillance unless in pursuit of a foreign connection to the group. No group shall be penetrated by Government agents, informants or others seeking to discredit or interrupt their meetings. The American people are not the proper target for such acts on the part of Government and no Government department, agent or investigative group, including the CIA and the FBI, shall ascribe motives to any group of citizens exercising this right. No court, including the Supreme Court, shall hear any case challenging this Amendment.

Each State shall have the right to control entry into its borders by roadway, seaports and airports, by foreign automobiles, trucks, buses, ships, airplanes or any other means of conveyance. The States shall have the right to fix entry fees or duties as they deem appropriate. No such fees or duties shall be applied to vehicles, vessels and airplanes of United States registry. No court, including the Supreme Court shall hear any case challenging these laws or this Amendment.

The Congress of the United States shall write no law permitting the extended families of immigrants to enter this country. No court, including the Supreme Court, shall hear cases brought to challenge this law or this Amendment.

The Congress shall write no law that provides amnesty to aliens living illegally in the United States. Illegal aliens, when found, shall be deported at once. There shall be no hearings attached to such action. No court, including the Supreme Court, shall hear any case challenging this law or this Amendment.

The Congress shall write no law permitting private citizens, corporations or other organizations, including religious, to induce illegal immigrants to enter the United States. Violation of this Amendment shall be cause for the organization being banned in the United States or loss of citizenship of the private individual involved. No court, including the Supreme Court, shall hear any case challenging this law or this Amendment.

No person of religion, based in a foreign land shall enter the United States, or be transferred to any State for any reason, without the express permission of the Federal Government, and the Government of the State of destination. All such persons must be fluent in English and undergo investigation by the Justice Department, the FBI and the CIA, before entering the United States, and shall be of good character and of no danger to any American citizen. Violation of this Amendment shall be cause for banishment of the religious organization from the United States. No court, including the Supreme Court, shall hear any case challenging any laws or any part of this amendment including the Amendment itself.

Religious organizations, and their affiliates, shall not interfere in the political process in America. No religious leader, organization, or its affiliates, may instruct their followers how to vote, or demand their votes in support of any candidate or political position or political party. Religious organizations shall remain distant from politics at every level in the United States. No court, including the Supreme Court shall hear any case challenging any law associated with this Amendment, or the Amendment itself.

The Congress shall write a law, or laws, making English the official language of the United States. No other language shall be used or published in the conduct of official business of the several states, at any level, as well as the Federal Government. No school, college or university, private, public or religious, shall be excepted. No court, including the Supreme Court, shall hear any case challenging this law or this Amendment.

No political, religious or other organization shall teach hatred of other individuals, people, organizations or religions in any manner. Violation of this Amendment shall be cause for banishment of these organizations from the United State. No court, including the Supreme Court may hear any case challenging this Amendment.

Religious organizations shall respect the privacy and property rights of individuals throughout the Land. Religious organizations their members or their representatives shall not trespass on private property without permission, under any circumstances. No court, including the Supreme Court, shall hear any case challenging this Amendment.

The Congress shall write a law suspending all immigration for a period of ten years, and at intervals of ten years afterward, for a period of five years. Illegal immigration shall be banned in perpetuity. No Court, including the Supreme Court shall hear cases challenging or altering this law or this Amendment.

Congress shall make no law that permits the President to declare war or take military action without a full declaration of war from the Congress, voted upon by all members of both houses. No court, including the Supreme Court, shall hear any case challenging this Amendment.

The Congress shall make no law permitting the President to use the military forces of the United States against the American people for any reason. No court, including the Supreme court, may hear any case challenging this Amendment.

No governor of any state shall use any military force, including the state national guard, to suppress the actions of the people for any reason. No court, including the Supreme Court, shall hear any case challenging this Amendment.

The Congress shall create a law entitled The Commercial Equalization Act, which shall require all retailers in the United States, selling foreign made products, to sell American made products of equal manufacture. Failure to comply with this law shall be cause for a fine equal to the annual value of the products sold. A second violation shall be cause for banishment of the organization from the United States. No court, including the Supreme Court, shall hear any case challenging this law or this Amendment.

Political parties shall not, in collusion with another political party act to establish election laws, filing requirements or in any other way fix or limit the ability of parties or candidates to run, campaign, and debate for office. The Federal Election Commission shall be eliminated with the passage of this Amendment. All campaign and elections laws in the various states shall be uniform in their application as defined by Congress. No Court, including the Supreme Court shall hear any case challenging any portion of the election laws or this Amendment.

No television network, cable network, TV or radio station, shall establish rules for coverage of any political candidate, or campaign that will exclude any candidate from the election process, on pain of loss of licenses under which they operate. Coverage of one, shall require coverage of all in equal measure, in manner of coverage and time of coverage. No court, including the Supreme Court shall hear any case challenging any aspect of this amendment.

No television network, radio or TV station shall deny air time to one candidate in favor of others. Coverage of one requires coverage of all. Time of coverage shall be equal in each case. No court, including the Supreme Court, shall hear any case challenging this Amendment.

Corporations with a net worth of more than a million dollars shall limit compensation of its executives to not more than 1 million dollars each. Such executives shall not be indemnified against legal action brought by any employee or stockholder, or member of the public. No court, including the Supreme Court shall hear any case challenging this Amendment.

Members of the Board of Directors of any corporation of any size shall not sit on any other board during or for ten years after the term of their employment. No court, including the Supreme Court shall hear any case challenging this Amendment.

No banker or associate or employee of a banker shall sit on any Board of Directors.

Corporations with a net worth of 1-100,000,000 dollars shall not cause their employees to work more than 40 hours in one week, without overtime pay of time and one half. Workers employed as supervisors shall not work more than 45 hours a week without overtime pay of time and one half. Supervisory employees performing routine work that is performed by non-supervisory employees shall be reclassified to regular employee status, and compensated as such. Extended work hours shall not be compulsory in any corporation. Employees of any corporation of 1 million to 1 hundred million dollars of net worth shall receive all benefits, including vacation and holidays, enjoyed by federal employees. All employees shall work no less than 40 hours in one week. All employees shall be considered permanent, full time employees. No court, including the Supreme Court shall hear any case challenging any aspect of this Amendment or the Amendment itself.

Executives of any corporation compensated at 1 million dollars shall pay a tax of 95 percent to the federal Government. No other compensation of any kind shall be extended to any officer of the corporation. No court, including the Supreme Court shall hear any case challenging any aspect of this Amendment or the Amendment itself.

No American Citizen shall hold accounts in any foreign banks. Failure to comply with this amendment is sufficient cause for loss of citizenship. No court, including the Supreme Court shall hear any case challenging this Amendment.

No treaty negotiated by the United States Government shall become the law of the land for a period of ten years, until the people determine that the treaty is to their liking. A national referendum on each such treaty shall be held at the next national election after the ten years have elapsed. No court, including the Supreme Court shall hear any case challenging this Amendment.

No post office of the United States, or other company, corporation or organization, including religious, shipping packages or mail of any kind, shall accept cash, money orders or other documents intended for payment in a foreign country. No embassy or mission of a foreign nation shall ship cash by means of diplomatic pouch, courier, or other means, into or out of the United States. Violation of this Amendment shall be cause for closure of the Embassy or mission of the country involved. No court, including the Supreme Court shall hear any case challenging this Amendment.

No department of the Government, including the Executive Department, shall originate and execute any rules and regulations that the Congress has refused to implement. Executive Orders that infringe upon the responsibilities of the Congress shall be unconstitutional. Violation of this Amendment shall be cause for impeachment of the Chief Executive. No court, including the Supreme Court shall hear any case challenging this Amendment.

No officer of the Government, including the President and the military leaders of the Armed Forces of the United States, shall take any action against the people when they are clearly in revolt against the Government. The people have an absolute right to throw off any Government they do not support. No court, including the Supreme Court shall hear any case challenging this Amendment.

The Congress of the United States shall write and pass laws that prohibit the support of any nation that belongs to or supports the International Criminal Court. No organization advocating support of the ICC shall be permitted to function within the United States. Violation of these laws shall be cause for loss of citizenship and exile of those involved. No court, including the Supreme Court shall hear any case challenging these laws or this Amendment.

The United Nations, being a world Government shall be identified as an enemy state, since its projected powers are in direct conflict with the Constitution of the United States. No American citizen shall support in any manner the creation of a world Government superior to the United States Government. The Congress of the United States shall write laws that prohibit the expenditure of any funds in support of the UN, and that outlaw this organization within the borders of the United States. The State Department and all federal offices shall have no contact with members of the UN and the armed forces of the United States shall eject the UN and all its members from the United States. Any citizen of the United States supporting the UN shall be declared a tergiversator, a renegade, and shall forfeit his citizenship in the United States and be forced to enter exile. The United Nations building in New York, shall be cleared of all foreign diplomats and their staff, and the building taken by the federal Government. It shall either be sold or destroyed and the land sold to the highest bidder. No court, including the Supreme Court, shall hear any case challenging any aspect of these laws or this Amendment.

The Congress shall appropriate funds for all elections and shall be sufficient for a two-month campaign using a combination of advertisements and television time. Equal support shall be assigned to challenger and incumbent. No other outside funds shall be accepted by any candidate and no person or organization shall provide any financial or other support. The Congress shall write laws making such support illegal and provide for severe penalties in each case. All election cycles shall be held within a two month period. No court, including the Supreme Court, shall hear any case challenging any portion of these laws and this Amendment.

Each television network, including cable networks and all TV stations shall provide air time for both candidates. Such time shall be equal for each candidate, and no TV station shall provide coverage for a candidate without providing the same coverage for the challenger. All networks and TV stations shall provide coverage as a condition of retaining their licenses to operate on the airwaves of the nation. No court, including the Supreme Court, shall hear any case challenging this law or this Amendment.

The right of American citizens to read any material, book, newspaper, or any other form of communications, view any form of entertainment, movies, videos, videotapes, etc, and to possess them for their education or information or any other reason, shall be inviolate. Possession of such materials is of no concern to the Government, other individuals, corporations, employers, or religious organizations or their followers, and interference of this right by anyone is unconstitutional. Violation of this Amendment shall be cause for a fine of 500,000 dollars and twenty years in prison for each case. No court, including the Supreme Court, shall hear any case challenging any portion of this Amendment or the Amendment itself.

No person employed by any stockbroker, mortgage company, or financial institution, shall induce another person to invest in any manner, where fraud, false information or other devious methods are involved. No court, including the Supreme Court, shall hear any case challenging this Amendment.

No village, town or city in the United States, no Government, State, local or federal agency shall place the American people under routine surveillance for any reason, including surveillance cameras in public areas, streets or other areas where people gather. Traffic surveillance cameras are specifically forbidden, since they are more a money raising device than a security device. This Amendment shall not be construed to prohibit investigation where there is evidence of a foreign influence, financial support or other foreign connections. No court, including the Supreme Court, shall hear any case challenging this Amendment.

No village, town or city in the United States, no Government, State local or federal, shall establish any law, rule or regulation that inhibits the establishment of any business. No fees or licenses shall be established covering new startup businesses, and such businesses shall be free of all regulatory agencies, including the IRS, for the first five years, and/or the first ten million dollars of income. No court, including the Supreme Court, shall hear any case challenging this provisions of this Amendment, or the Amendment itself.

No candidate for the Presidency, shall name a spouse, relative or friend as a running mate for the Vice-presidency, or any other seat in the House of Representatives or the Senate. No political party shall attempt to do the same. So-called "two for one" candidacies are specifically forbidden, and shall be unconstitutional. No spouse may sit in any chamber of the Government, or have any official or unofficial duties, or draw any federal pay or have an office within the Government while married to a President or President-elect. No court, including the Supreme Court shall hear any case challenging any aspect of this Amendment or the Amendment itself.

The President, Vice President and members of the House and Senate shall take office immediately upon election to their office. Lame duck presidencies and Congresses shall be unconstitutional. No court, including the Supreme Court shall hear any case challenging this Amendment.

Upon election to any office in the United States, federal, state or local, the winning candidate shall disclose his net worth to the applicable State or federal accounting office. Such information shall be published in newspapers and on television networks or stations for at least ten days. Upon leaving office, the assets of the office holder shall be no greater than the amount declared upon entering office. Any amount greater, shall be forfeit to the United States Treasury, or the applicable Government treasury. No political office, including the Presidency, shall be exempt from this requirement. No court, including the Supreme Court, shall hear any case challenging any aspect of this Amendment, or the Amendment itself.

No newspaper or other publisher or television network or TV station, including cable networks shall publish or broadcast news stories without a valid source. Blind sources, such as "critics say-, others indicate," etc. are specifically forbidden. News items shall be clearly identified as news. Opinion pieces must be clearly identified. No court, including the Supreme Court, shall hear any case challenging this Amendment.

News reporters of all kinds, print or electronic media, shall be licensed by the state after graduation from a University school of Journalism which has included courses on ethics. No less than a Bachelor's degree in Journalism shall be required for such license. An individual who has labored in the news business for a period for at least seven years shall also qualify for such license without a degree. No fee shall be attached to this license. No court, including the Supreme Court, shall hear any case challenging this Amendment.

All television networks, TV stations, and radio broadcasters in the United States shall broadcast in English. Those stations previously broadcasting in other languages shall within one year, broadcast ten percent in English. Within three years, they shall broadcast in English fifty percent of the time. Within five years such stations shall broadcast only in English. No court, including the Supreme Court, shall hear any case challenging this Amendment.

Each college or University shall identify the President and all other senior executives controlling the school. All faculty professors or other persons teaching at the school, shall be identified and the school shall publish the information annually. Each school executive and faculty member shall be alphabetically listed, along with his educational background, nationality, and membership in private organizations. If a foreigner, additional information shall be added outlining his political leanings. No court, including the Supreme Court, shall hear any case challenging this Amendment.

No corporation or business organization shall operate with fraudulent practices as a part of their service. Conviction of fraud shall be cause for the termination of the business or Corporation, imprisonment of the officers and board members of the Corporation or business for not less than ten years, and fine of fifty to five hundred thousand dollars, depending on the size of the business. Corporations of any size, (more than 200 employees), shall receive the maximum penalty. No court, including the Supreme Court, shall hear any case challenging any aspect of this Amendment, or the Amendment itself.

No Corporation shall extend any loans to their chief executives, or any senior staff members or board members.

Those compensated at a million dollars per year shall pay an excess profits tax of at least 95%. No court, including the Supreme Court, shall hear any case challenging any aspect of this Amendment or the Amendment itself.

No bank or other financial institution in the United States shall charge an interest rate of more than 6%. No bank or other financial institution shall offer a credit card to anyone under twenty-one years of age. No bank or financial institution shall charge more than 6% interest annually on any credit card. Credit cards shall be issued only to individuals who request them, and who have passed a credit check. No bank shall charge any fee upon withdrawal of personal funds. No court, including the Supreme Court, shall hear any case challenging any aspect of this Amendment or the Amendment itself.

No person or organization in the U. S. shall fly any flag except the American flag. Flags of other countries may be flown, temporarily, at ceremonial occasions, during daylight hours. No foreign flag shall be flown under any circumstances, for more than 24 hours. The flag of the United Nations shall not be flown under any circumstances, at any time. No court, including the Supreme Court, shall hear any case challenging this Amendment.

Every person having been granted the status of a naturalized American Citizen shall hold that status only after demonstrating satisfactory behavior for a period of ten years. If, during that period the naturalized Citizen is found to have been involved in any illegal acts or crimes, he shall have his naturalized Citizen status revoked and be immediately deported to his home country after completing any prison term applied. No hearing shall be provided, and he may not be again provided any status permitting him to visit, emigrate to or remain in the United States. The Immigration and Naturalization Service of the federal Government shall register and track the whereabouts of each naturalized citizen for ten years, and shall be advised of any arrests sustained by the provisional citizen during that period. No court, including the Supreme Court shall hear any case challenging any aspect of this Amendment, or the Amendment itself.

No woman who is pregnant upon arrival in the United States shall be permitted to remain in the United States, but must be deported to her home country immediately. There shall be no hearing in this matter. No court, including the Supreme Court shall hear any case challenging this Amendment.

No State nor Congress shall write laws that extend American law beyond the borders of the United States. No court, including the Supreme Court shall hear any case challenging this Amendment.

Neither the United States nor any State shall make an international agreement that has the effect of nullifying or changing the laws of the United States or of the several States or the Constitution of the United States, nor shall it conclude any international agreement that has any affect on the citizens of the United States. No court, including the Supreme Court shall hear any case challenging this Amendment.

No foreign law, including those of the United Nations, shall apply within the borders of the United States, nor shall they have any applicability to United States citizens under any circumstances. United States citizens are the Sovereigns of the United States and as such are heads of state immune to laws of foreign states and entities. No court, including the Supreme Court, or courts of other nations or the United Nations, shall hear any case challenging any part of this Amendment or the Amendment itself. All foreign laws, from any source, are unconstitutional and without affect.

The United States shall break diplomatic relations with any country that acts as an enemy of the United States or its people. Countries that teach their children that the US is an enemy or evil, or is in any other way an undesirable country shall not be given diplomatic entry into the United States. Diplomatic opposition and all other negative relations with such countries shall be applied in full, and no benefit to the country involved shall accrue. No US funds from the federal treasury or any other source shall be sent to such countries either directly or indirectly through other countries or channels. Violations of these provisions shall be cause for impeachment of the President and discharge of any federal employee involved as well as ten years imprisonment and a fine of one Million dollars. No court, including the Supreme Court shall hear any case challenging this Amendment.

The United States Government and each of the several states shall take no position on the subject of abortion or reproductive rights, or any associated subject, domestically or internationally. Such rights do not fall within the purview of the Government. The American people possess all rights, including that of abortion and reproductive rights and no person, organization or association, including religious, shall take any action to prevent the exercise of such actions or rights in the United States. Violation of this Amendment, in each case, shall be cause for a fine of 500,000 dollars and imprisonment of ten years. No court, including the Supreme Court, shall hear any case challenging any portion of such rights, or any part of this Amendment, or the Amendment itself.

The reproductive and privacy rights of American women shall begin at age twelve, and no female having attained that age shall be denied full access to non-religious reproductive counseling, birth control information and medications, and family planning counseling, by any person or religious organization, including parents of the female. Parental control of such rights shall be advisory only. No medical professional person or hospital shall refuse to provide counseling to such females on demand. Violation of this Amendment shall be cause for a fine of a half million dollars and a prison term of not less than ten years for each case. An additional fine of one million dollars shall be levied against any religious organization or member of such organization interfering in any way with the abortion or reproductive rights of any female. No court, including the

Supreme Court shall hear any case challenging any aspect of this Amendment, or the Amendment itself.

The federal Government and each of the State Governments shall not take any position officially or unofficially on the subject of abortion or reproductive rights, nor shall they support any position or religious pronouncements on these subjects, including messages on license plates which shall be banned nationwide. Violation of this Amendment shall be cause for prosecution of each person involved, including federal, state and local officials, religious leaders and followers, and require a prison term of not less than thirty years, and a fine of five million dollars, in each case. An additional fine of ten million dollars shall be assessed against any religious organization involved in each case. No court, including the Supreme Court, shall hear any case challenging any part of this Amendment, or the Amendment itself.

No religious organization, officials of such organizations or followers of such organizations shall take any action to influence the votes or other actions of any federal, state or local official in the performance of their official duties, or cause them to make public statements regarding the right of any other person to engage in any activity they choose in the matter of abortion, or reproductive rights. No court, including the Supreme Court, shall hear any case challenging this Amendment or any portion of this Amendment.

All corporate assets shall be prevented from being moved overseas to any country, competitor, subsidiary entity, bank or financial institution. Violation of this Amendment shall be cause for a fine of not less than 100 percent of the total value of the Corporation and a prison term of not less than twenty years for the chief executive and board members of the corporation. A second violation shall be cause for forfeiture of the Corporation to the United States Government, and imprisonment of the Board of Directors for not less than twenty-five years. No court, including the Supreme Court, shall hear any case challenging any part of this Amendment or the Amendment itself.

No school in the United States shall teach a foreign language to its students until they have reached the age of twenty one and are enrolled in a foreign service or diplomatic service career course. Bilingual education is specifically forbidden in all schools and colleges. Foreign languages shall be taught only at the post graduate level in the United States. No court, including the Supreme Court shall hear any case challenging this Amendment.

No person shall control or be a part of any financial institution of any kind without his connection to such institutions being published by the federal Government or the State in which the institution is located. No such person shall have access to or control any other financial institution, nor shall he sit on any board of directors of any financial institution. No court, including the Supreme Court shall hear any case challenging any part of this Amendment.

In a case of public corruption, or misbehavior of any public official at any level, there shall be no statute of limitation applied by any court, including the Supreme Court. The Congress and the various legislatures shall not create or pass any law that provides a statute of limitations for such cases. No court, including the Supreme Court, shall hear any case challenging this Amendment.

All records, whether paper, electronic or other, generated or originated during any political administration of the Government, are and shall remain the property of the people and retained, in unclassified status, for all time in the National Archives or archives of the applicable State. No Government employee, including those of the Executive Department and the President or Vice President, shall take custody of such papers for more than a time sufficient for accomplishment of current duties. Such papers or records shall not be destroyed under any circumstance. Violation of this Amendment shall be cause for a fine of one million dollars and twenty five years imprisonment for each case. No court, including the Supreme Court shall hear any case challenging any portion of this Amendment, or the Amendment itself.

The United States Government shall not contract out or permit any private or educational organization to manage secret research facilities where classified projects are being conducted or developed. No University or other educational institution or its students shall be permitted access to such facilities, nor shall any faculty member or student of any University or College be permitted access to secret, top secret or Restricted (nuclear) Data of any kind. No Government employee except the President shall have access to such facilities and data. All such management and access shall fall within the purview of the appropriate United States Military Organizations. Foreign nationals are specifically forbidden to have access to such data, or work at or visit such facilities. The Military forces of the United States are forbidden from contracting out such work or program to any foreign or domestic source. No court, including the Supreme Court shall hear any case challenging this Amendment, or any provision thereof.

Transmittal or provision of access to any classified material by any person, including members of any branch of Government, to unauthorized persons or newspersons shall be a violation of this Amendment and punishable by a prison term of not less that twenty five years and a fine of one million dollars for both the transmitter and recipient of the information. Transmission of such data or information to foreigners by any military officer, shall be punishable on conviction, by execution. No court, including the Supreme Court, shall hear any case challenging any provision of this Amendment or the Amendment itself.

No foreign surveillance or intelligence service, of any State or country, shall operate within the United States or any of its possessions. Violation of this Amendment shall be cause for execution of the Intelligence officer involved, without trial, and a fine of fifty million dollars for the country involved, and the termination of Diplomatic relations with that country. No court, including the Supreme Court, shall hear any case challenging this Amendment.

No corporation or other organization operating in the United States shall seek employees in another nation, either to come to the United States for employment, or for employment in their own country to provide support of any kind, technical or simply advice, to customers in the United States via telephone or any other communication device. Corporations violating this Amendment shall be fined not less that one million dollars per incident and their CEO imprisoned for not less than twenty years. No court, including the Supreme Court shall hear any case challenging this Amendment or any portion of this Amendment.

No school, College or University, including graduate school, or any other educational institution, private or public, shall use any criterion for admission or advancement, or any other change in status of students, other than merit. No other objective shall be used, including diversity or any other social criteria, in deciding the admission, advancement or any other status of any student. No court, including the Supreme Court, shall hear any case challenging any part of this Amendment, or the Amendment itself.

No criteria except merit shall be applied in any choice of persons for employment, or reduction in employment, in any business operating in the United States. Employers violating this Amendment shall be fined not less than a million dollars in each incident and the owner/operator or the CEO and Board members shall be imprisoned for a term of at least ten years. No court, including the Supreme Court shall hear any case challenging this Amendment.

No foreign Government shall be permitted to establish any embassy, legation or other office representing their Government in the United States, except their Embassy in Washington D.C. Foreign Governments attempting to establish such offices in the United States shall be expelled from the United States, and the offices involved shall be closed by the Armed Forces of the United States or of the

State where such offices might exist, and their diplomats and other workers expelled from the US without a hearing of any kind. State officials are fully empowered to take action to expel diplomats and close such offices at will. No court, including the Supreme Court shall hear any case challenging this Amendment, and no office of the federal Government shall attempt to thwart this Amendment.

No corporation shall own, operate or own stock in or in any way control another domestic or international corporation, whether within its own field or not. Corporations known as conglomerates shall be specifically forbidden, and must be broken up when discovered. Violation of this Amendment shall be cause for imprisonment of the Officers and board members of the corporation for a period of not less than fifty years and each fined not less than ten million dollars. No court, including the Supreme Court, shall hear any case challenging any portion of this Amendment, or the Amendment itself.

No person or group of persons shall own or direct a corporation or other organization in the newspaper, electronic media or other news or entertainment dissemination field, which controls other such outlets. Control of single newspapers and TV stations shall be limited to one corporation and limited to one city. The broadcast power of such TV stations shall be limited such that the signal covers the general area of the city only and in no case shall reach more than forty miles from the broadcast tower. This Amendment shall not be construed to limit the number of separately owned outlets in any one city or area. No court, including the Supreme Court, shall hear any case challenging this Amendment or any part of this Amendment.

No corporation, corporate officer or manager shall reduce or make any use of the retirement benefits accruing for the employees of the corporation. Misuse, misappropriation, theft, diversion or dissolution of such benefits, retirement funds or other funds intended for eventual payment to the employees shall be a major felony punishable by fifty years in prison and a fine of ten million dollars. In addition, the corporation shall pay a fine of not less than the intended total accrued value of the pension fund. Persons convicted of such acts shall not subsequently hold a position of trust in any corporation in the United States. No court, including the Supreme Court shall hear any case challenging this amendment.

No infant shall be identified as a person until that infant has reached the point of development that will allow it to live and breathe on its own outside and unconnected to the mother for at least 24 hours. Other than providing food and water, no medical doctor or other medical professional shall during the 24 hour period take any heroic action to cause the infant to extend its life more than it would live on its own. No court, including the Supreme Court shall hear any case challenging this Amendment.

No person, medical doctor or any other medical professional or organization shall perform an abortion after the fetus has developed identifiable limbs and live movements. Violation of this Amendment is punishable by a prison term of not more than five years in prison and a fine of five thousand dollars. No person, organization or member of such organization, including religious, shall act in any way to prevent an abortion before the fetus has developed identifiable limbs and live movements. Violation of this Amendment shall be punishable by a fine of not less that one million dollars and imprisonment of the perpetrator for a period of not less than ten years. A religious organization violating this Amendment shall pay a fine of not less than twenty million dollars and the leader of the organization shall be imprisoned for not less that twenty years. No court, including the Supreme Court shall hear any case challenging any portion of this Amendment or the Amendment itself.

No Government, federal, state or local, shall pass any law or regulation limiting sexual activity of any kind, between consenting individuals, regardless of the ages of the persons involved. No court, including the Supreme Court shall hear any case challenging this Amendment.

A Constitutional Convention is a major undertaking by whoever calls it and it should not be contemplated lightly. It will be tumultuous at times, and many hours will be expended in arguments by many individuals, but in the end, agreement will prevail. Fifty five men argued during the first Constitutional Convention, and even then, three members would not sign it. Yet it has stood for two hundred twenty six years, a testament to their foresight and intelligence, and their dogged determination to make this country work for the people.

One might wonder why the first Constitutional Convention did not include more specific language to combat what even then might have been foreseen as trouble points. The answer is that they were afraid to include anything that might inhibit the chances of the new Government to succeed, or certainly we would not have had the two hundred twenty six years of a Republic that we have enjoyed. Now, however, there are many causes of uncertainty and danger to our Republic. They must be addressed in no uncertain terms. To aid in this process, it is recommended that the Second Constitutional Convention be held in the center of the land, and not in Washington, D.C, or New York. It is recommended that a suitable facility be found in St. Louis or Kansas City.

You should strive to make our new Constitution even better than the original. But be very careful of those who would lead it astray. They must not prevail. Listen to your hearts. You will know what to do. The new America must be more American than ever before. And more free than ever before.

# CHAPTER 23

## HOW CORPORATIONS EXPAND
## THEIR POWER & INFLUENCE

Wherever Corporations are located in the United States, their reason for existing is to make money. Some have, over the years, been remarkably successful. Many Corporations now have a net worth that exceeds by far, the total economic value of many countries. Accordingly their power to influence Governments is vast. But great mischief can be rendered by those who run Corporations, the Board of Directors. (It should be noted here that we are talking about large Corporations, not small ones.)

Corporations are organized under laws governing such enterprises. In most cases, the number of Directors to make up the Board is dictated either the law covering such matters or the bylaws of the Corporation itself. Ordinarily, all Board members are indemnified against penalty as a result of their actions, unless those actions are unlawful. Board members are usually installed either as a replacement or as a new Board member either by a vote of the shareholders or by a vote of the Board itself.

There are no laws that prevent a Board member from sitting on more than one Board and therein lies an unrecognized problem. Suppose, for instance a Board member of Corporation A is invited to become a Board member of Corporation B, but he is a friend of or former employee of Corporation C. This board member can vote for actions at A and B that benefit C. legally, and without the knowledge of anyone at A or B. Board members often sit on many Boards simultaneously. Most are compensated generously for their work. Many well known politicians and others in Washington and New York sit on many boards of major Corporations, Tax free Foundations, etc.

What most people do not recognize about Corporations is that the deck is stacked in their favor. Deliberately. No such advantage is found on the other side of the equation, Labor. And it's all legal. It's not right, but it's legal. Several reasons are responsible for their good fortune.

They are: Lobbying. Lobbyists working for Corporations with many resources dispense money to the corrupt politicians in Government, who vote for programs benefiting the Corporation. In other words, your politicians take bribes. Such bribes are received under the general heading of campaign finance contributions. Politicians do not see themselves as corrupt. The average man would call him a crook.

# CHAPTER 24

## ARE WE MORALLY BANKRUPT-HEADED TO HELL IN A HANDBASKET?

Many otherwise sensible people are convinced that America's future is dark; that the youth of today is headed in a self-indulgent and hedonistic direction. If this were not so laughable, it would be disturbing. But this perception of where we are going is flawed. It is the vision of little minds.

In the nineteen twenties, some in our society were shaken by the appearance of the Flappers, young women who exhibited themselves and their assets publicly and with abandon. The same thing was said in those days-that we were headed to Hell. In WW I, before the twenties, there was even a song written about "How are you gonna keep them down on the farm when they've seen Paree?" It was and is laughable, but some segments of our society worried that the morals of Paris would somehow corrupt our young soldiers. But Paris is Paris and with its looseness and wild women, it is still functioning. And our boys learned nothing they didn't already know during their time in Paris.

Our young people of today are smarter, freer and healthier in many ways than our young people have ever been. Of course they are quite familiar with the seamier side of life. They see it on TV every day. They are acquainted with all the methods of sexual gratification at an earlier age than ever before. And Mother Nature is keeping pace. Young girls are now going through puberty at an earlier age, and boys are keeping pace with the girls.

It is the height of foolishness to worry about where we are heading morally. We will arrive at our destined location and status when it is appropriate to do so. And we will arrive as free Americans, our eyes on the stars as always, visions in our minds of greater achievements than our parents dreamed of.

In 1880, the age of consent in New York City was nine. By 1900 it had risen to age 12. And so on. Were our fathers and grandfathers more enlightened than we thought? Were they already more tolerant than we think? Did they know Mother Nature better than we do?

The point is, that society somehow listened to those who decry instead of those who exult in the wonders of life. The decriers are still out there, but youths are not listening. Nor should they. Life is for the adventurous. It should be lived with a lusty fervor, and the hell with the frowns! Still, our youths must be wary of big Government. And they are. More and more each year they are aware of the hazards of globalism and corporate excesses. And they are rebelling. That can only be good for our national future.

Finally, it is with amusement that we learn that oldsters in retirement villages in Arizona are having sex in public places. Some things never change, they just go public. Relax and enjoy life. There never has been a country as wonderful as the United States, and there never will be. We will be the same for a thousand years. We're not going to Hell in a hand basket; we're just reinventing ourselves and our future! And the stars are in our future! Reagan, the man who killed the Soviet Union saw that clearly. He never looked back. Nor should we.

# CHAPTER 25

## THE WORLD BANK &
## INTERNATIONAL MONEY FUND

During periods of strife or war, those organizations and individuals, including those in Government, who are interested in secretly making changes in the way the Government operates, are exceedingly active. The conflicts taking place serve to distract the people's attention, and the history of the Government's subversive activities in wartime is an unsavory one. The war is prosecuted, of course, but behind the scenes, mischief- making is rampant.

The World Bank, and its sister organization, the IMF, came into being in 1944 during World War II when nearly 13 Million American men were fighting for their country. Those on the home front were busy building the materials their soldiers, sailors and airmen needed, and their attention was diverted away from the treachery that was taking place in Washington.

What was happening was the purposeful intent of elitists and globalists to create an Unconstitutional system whereby third world countries could be brought into the twentieth century, economically speaking, and which they would control. The system was designed by dilettantes and sycophants in the Treasury Department, at the behest of the Secretary of the Treasury. What resulted was the creation of the United Nations, the World Bank and the IMF, which depended solely on the contribution of tax money from the member states. Of course, the United States, being the world leader even in those days, had to be the largest contributor.

The average citizen, whose native instincts would have rejected the proposed system out of hand, would never have dreamed of the proposed foolishness to come. It was if the dumbest people in the world were designing the World Bank and the International Money Fund. It has always been a fact of life that one cannot lend money to someone who has no means of repayment of the loan. The plan ignored such trifles and went forward, with the President pushing it into being through an Executive Order, an unconstitutional act.

The result was inevitable. The history of the Bank and IMF over decades of their existence has been a dismal failure, and in fact more than ample evidence has existed for years that these two agencies should be defunded at once. Yet the Government persists in supporting them. The American people have been fleeced to the tune of billions of dollars for this deceptive and unconstitutional program.

It is not surprising therefore, to learn that the history of banking in the world, is one of periodic failures, overextensions and collapses. It is these perturbations in the banking system that the Government sought to control over the years with a minimum of publicity, lest a run on the banks get out of hand. To do this they created the Federal Reserve System and the Federal Deposit Insurance System.

The World Bank, the IMF and its sister organizations must be stopped in their tracks and put out of business for good. We simply can't afford their foolish plans any longer.

# CHAPTER 26

## THE POLITICAL LEFT AND RIGHT

The terms of political identity have changed over the years. The lines of demarcation used to be fairly clear, but modern politics have blurred the center, while markedly changing the extremes, right and left, with values most abhor. Because most people are in the center, or nearly so, people in this situation are dismayed by what has been happening. Most people in this country are more Conservative than Liberal. Yet most are pro-choice on abortion, quite liberal about sexual and other personal activities. (Contrary to some views, this is not a liberal political stance at all but one of tolerance.) Most of these same people are fiscal conservatives. The political left is occupied by a distinct minority, however vocal they may be. Their actual voice is magnified by a sympathetic media, which is itself left-leaning.

The modern political left has become less of a bomb-throwing crowd than it was a few years ago, but is much more vitriolic in its ascription of traits to its opposite character, the political right. Character assassination is its main tool. Its most used secondary tool is the boycott, or accusations made to the most vulnerable supporters of the right such as employers and or companies that are perceived to be supporting the right. The Media, Hollywood and colleges and universities, the modern captives of the looney Liberals, are their great allies in pressing their case for their beliefs.

The modern political right is no better than the left. It has its own radical agitators in the churches of the country, (the crazy conservatives) and is just as vociferous as their leftist counterparts. They are more supported on talk radio than the left, but are even uglier in their beliefs about those who do not subscribe to their views. They have not yet begun to display the viciousness of their attacks on others that the left has, but they are not far behind.

We believe in free speech for everyone in this country, but extreme elements of the political left and right do not, and are doing everything they can to keep people from expressing their ideas if they differ from their own. This is profoundly un-American, and really hated by most in the middle. Somehow, the extremes must be stopped. Their activities are not healthy for this country.

# CHAPTER 27

## THE PROPAGANDISTS

Americans today realize that they are under constant domestic propaganda attacks by those who hate America and those who want to change America. Most of these attacks come from the Universities and colleges of this country, but are assisted mightily by the media, Hollywood, and a myriad of entities and radicals abroad in the country, who are essentially extreme left politically. Their targets are the young people, whose attitudes and beliefs can still be changed and molded to suit their purposes. The elderly, who fought fascism and communism earlier in their lives, are not through fighting yet. They must yet fight the greatest battle of their lives; historical revisionists and the authors of political correctness, the most destructive of all elements working to change America forever. These are the proponents of "dumbing down America".

The elderly and parents of young people about to enter our universities must prepare their young to recognize the propaganda they are about to encounter in the edifices of higher learning and to pay no attention to it, marginalize it and reject it completely. Of particular concern are professors of History and Sociology although many others are capable of leading youngsters astray.

It is essential to recognize that those in a position to influence others, particularly the young, usually have an agenda, a purpose behind their remarks. Few Americans realize that two of the three old network news anchors are members of the Council on Foreign Relations, and that those members use the CFR line when discussing much of the news. Some even use other members of the CFR as so called "experts", on some subject, usually dealing with foreign affairs. Unknowingly, you are being propagandized by your newscaster.

Other propagandists exist on television, including one retired news anchor who sonorously tells his listeners that

Americans must give up some of their sovereignty to achieve a "New World order." What garbage! This highly regarded individual once told his audience in all seriousness that the world was running out of oxygen! So much for those who would change us. Their opinions are no better than yours and should be given little regard. Your native intelligence will serve you best when something tells you that you should take with a grain of salt the words of those who try to persuade you to change your views on any given subject. Usually, your views are correct.

It is of major concern to Americans that the Government has permitted huge Corporations to gobble up most of the news organizations and television stations and networks in the United States. This process is still going on through mergers and acquisitions so that as time goes on, fewer and fewer people own or control more and more news outlets. This is a major achievement for those who would control us, and their propaganda is magnified a thousand-fold by such acquisitions. Yet it is all legal, although it should not be. Rule of thumb-don't believe every voice you hear or talking head you see on television.

# CHAPTER 28

## THE SEPARATION OF CHURCH AND STATE

Americans for nearly two hundred years have been very proud of the separation of Church and State that has been in existence in the United States. Freedom to worship as one chooses has bred tolerance for different religions for the same amount of time. Most American do not want to change that stance. But today there are those who want to end that tolerance, believing their own religion must prevail. And there are those without religion who want to use their non-beliefs to change the United States.

We are besieged by religion-based arguments in the mass media, particularly television, including those from politicians who firmly state that they will not vote for one position or another, that their individual religious beliefs prevent them from doing so. Nothing is said in regard to their being a Representative of voters back home, whose beliefs are the only ones that count. With that kind of representation, the people are voiceless. These "religious" Representatives should be judged unfit for public service, expelled from Congress and prevented from running for office again.

And there are those whose religious beliefs are rooted in violence or radical action as they combat a perceived wrong on the part of other religious people.

One can quickly understand that hardened positions on any question can initiate dangerous actions. This situation is relatively new in our country, and it is an ugly manifestation of beliefs strongly held.

We do not need a Christian Taliban movement in this country. Yet this is what is developing. We do not need a "Morals" police in this country. Yet that is what is happening. Those who are determined to control what others think are trying to become rulers of all. It is a righteous thing, according to the new Taliban believers, to keep people from thinking certain things, especially about sex. About what men and women do in the privacy of their homes. No, you just can't think any way you like, believe in what you want. Absolutely not, we won't allow that!

These people are determined to prevail in the name of their religion. But when will they require women to cover themselves in public? When will they begin to beat them with sticks? When will they begin to kill in the name of righteousness?

These are supposed to be Americans? If they are, they must be the sorriest individuals bred in this country in more than two hundred years.

Suppression of thought, the most repugnant of all restrictions on a free people cannot be tolerated. We do not need a Protestant Taliban, nor a Jewish Taliban. Nor a Catholic Taliban. Nor a Muslim Taliban. Or any other kind of Taliban. Such developments are the ugliest form of religious expression, and the most un-American activity that can be imagined.

All such developments must be fought by all Americans, regardless of religion and those who are involved should be ashamed of themselves and shunned by all true Americans.

Today, churches and other religious organizations are filled with zeal to impact the political process in America. The Catholic Church has a centuries old history of interference in social and political events around the world. In some countries, the function of the church is indistinguishable from the activities of the State. This activity in America is anathema to most Americans, who see no proper role for any church in public affairs, Catholic, Protestant or any other. Accordingly, to stop such interference in our political system, heavy taxes must be levied against the offending churches, and religious organizations. There should be a sliding scale of taxes, with the heaviest taxes levied against the most politically active church. If changes are not forthcoming, a Constitutional Amendment will be the only way to bring things under control. Eventually, the offending religions may well be banned from the United States. To not bring these problems under control may initiate the breakup of the Union.

# CHAPTER 29

## WHAT HAPPENED TO THE FBI AND THE CIA?

All Americans are astounded and dismayed at the activities, and lack thereof in our Security Services in the past decade. Despite the annual expenditure of billions of dollars for such services, we appear to be defenseless against the attacks of determined and aggressive terrorists. The reasons for their hatred of our country have been addressed in other parts of the Sovereign American. This essay is limited to the lack of efficiency of the FBI and the CIA.

As we see it, the culture of the FBI, pre September 11, 2001 was that of an entrenched beauracracy with nothing better to do than the occasional crime investigation, and a too- inquisitive attitude regarding what Americans were doing. They were wont to use unconstitutional procedures, where trumped up charges against an individual at Ruby Ridge were allowed to escalate into a series of FBI murders. They used military equipment and tactics to quell the acts of a single man and his family. Much of their tactics were later found to be unconstitutional and the Federal Government had to pay more than $3,000,000 in damages to the family that was attacked.

Not learning anything from Ruby Ridge, the FBI compounded its troubles at Waco, where their military tactics and equipment resulted in the fiery deaths of many men, women and children and the destruction of a church.

In fact, the pre September 11 stance of the FBI was little different than that of Hitler's Gestapo, with far too much concern about what American citizens were up to as opposed to the true enemies of the people who live and work in Washington and New York.

The American people are not and never have been the enemy, but even now, as this is written, the FBI is planning to greatly increase the surveillance of Americans. The Congress of the United States should come down hard on this plan and stop it in its tracks.

The CIA is an even greater enigma now, after 9-11-01, than it was before that date. It has had many failures and has been penetrated by the Russians like a piece of swiss cheese. We certainly do not get what we pay for with this outfit.

Apparently, both the FBI and the CIA have an entrenched culture of arrogance and unaccountability which generates an attitude of "I know best", and "you have no need to know what I know." That was unacceptable in the past and is even more unacceptable now. Someone had better work out on these people. The current Congress and President are not the ones who can do the job. They have proved incompetent to handle the task.

# CHAPTER 30

## HOW THE AMERICAN PEOPLE WILL
## CHANGE AMERICA FOR GOOD

Every American knows that America must change politically. There are too many things wrong with our system to allow them to go unchanged much longer. But how will the people change the United States? It will be earthshaking!

We will eliminate massive international corporations that serve only their executives and a minority of their stockholders while amassing billions of dollars of net worth. The average American earns nothing in the way of income from these organizations. Even if he wanted to become a shareholder, the taxes he pays annually make it impossible for the average man or woman to make such an investment.

The great bulk of the American people are either nearly broke, or heavily in debt to banks and credit card companies who steal their money, unregulated by the federal Government.

What difference will it make to kill off these giant corporations? Very little, to the average man. After all, they pay few taxes to the Government, so you will not have to take up that slack. They have hordes of lawyers to keep them from paying taxes like the little man. And if they do pay taxes, they move offshore to Bermuda, or move their profits to subsidiaries overseas to further eliminate the taxes remaining.

If we kill them off or reduce them in size and power, and if we make lobbying a felony, they will not be able to employ their lobbyists, who control the Congress and Senate, who will in turn not be indebted to them for passing legislation the little man does not want anyway.

The average man would not know if General Motors, General Electric or Archer Daniels Midland existed or not. Smaller companies would take up the slack. We do not need big business. We need smaller corporations, millions upon millions of them, operating with no Government interference and hindrances.

We will stop the unconstitutional activities of Government by redefining the constitutional limits under which the Government operates. A part of that will be a new, more modern Constitution. We will criminalize the activities that our Representatives and Senators engage in if they are contrary to the new Constitution. And we will downsize the federal Government and put it into a Constitutional box that will prevent it for all time reconstituting itself in its present form. To accomplish this we will take many activities away from the federal Government and transfer them to the States. In fact, the very lifeblood of the federal Government, our tax money, will be drastically reduced and redirected to the States before it goes to the federal Government. And, we will make it impossible for the Federal Government to run a deficit in order to grow without the approval of the people.

We will redefine the role of the States within our Government, and we will make them superior to the federal Government except for national defense, Air Traffic Control, the Postal Service and Social Security, etc.

We will break the strangle hold that the great banks, the great corporations, the great universities and the wealthy elite in Washington and New York hold on the American people. It is this nexus that is the great enemy of all Americans. They keep the people in little more than poverty, and the greatest hazard to everyone who hopes to be free and able to take care of himself are the ruthless tentacles of the Federal Reserve and its chairman, scrooge himself reincarnated from fiction of old. He is the proverbial sleazy used car salesman from whom most citizens would shrink in disgust on meeting.

We will free the American people from their tax burden, and make foreign businesses and nations pay to replace the money that would otherwise be lost. We will free American businesses from the clutches of OSHA, the IRS, the EPA and all the other alphabet organizations that stifle new startups and kill them off within a year of their inception with miles of red tape. These are Liberal make-work ideas and organizations which serve no logical purpose except to eat out the substance of the people.

We will free the people from the incompetence of the Immigration and Naturalization Service, who have no stomach for apprehending and deporting those who do not belong in this country. We will stop all immigration for at least ten years, and periodically thereafter. We will require all foreigners in the United States to speak English in the business world, and we will require all broadcasting and official business of the States to be conducted only in English. Is this xenophobic? Not at all, Americans fear no foreigner, but foreigners must not be permitted to overrun and balkanize this nation. Foreigners who become immigrants to this Nation must understand that they must assimilate into the general population, not become part of a non-American sub-culture within the United States. They must understand that we will no longer tolerate foreign workers, legal and illegal, using this country as a milk cow, to send the bulk of their earnings back home, no matter how necessary they might feel that might be. Every dollar sent back to foreign nations by persons or businesses living and working here is a dollar not recycled here, and works against the interests of the American people.

We will make it possible for Americans to close the borders of their states to foreigners, their products and their influence, and control access to their states.

We will free the American people from the chains of an unconstitutional corporate Government that ships their jobs overseas in the name of free trade, and the tyranny of national retailers who sell only foreign made goods, where they pay wages so low that no American can compete in the resulting trade/wage imbalance.

We will free the American people from the insidious and destructive idea that the American people have a responsibility to other less fortunate peoples and countries around the world, and must invest untold billions of tax dollars in lifting these unfortunates out of their quagmire.

This is a liberal shibboleth intended to make liberals feel good. The real world dictates that such unfortunate people must do as we did, and revolt against the politicians and leaders that keep them from realizing their potential. It is not a problem that Americans should shoulder or pay for. It is a problem foreigners must solve for themselves.

We will make the rest of the world understand that the American people have no interest the future wellbeing of the many foreign states who look down their noses at us from their inflated egotistical views of their supposed political, intellectual and philosophical superiority. Americans have little patience with such pretenses and we will ensure that none of the hard earned tax dollars of the American people are sent to their shores. We will abandon NATO, and turn our backs on the Euro, as well as the European Union and the World Trade Organization and the World Court. We will have good relations with those States that have good relations with us. But we will tolerate no more turned up noses.

We will free the American people from the terribly divisive effect of the abortion question. Positions have hardened on this problem and the Government must take action to defuse this issue. The Government must codify and make safe the full rights of the women of America. They are half of the population and no stone must be left unturned in assuring their reproductive rights and their privacy. We will make the women of America whole again, full citizens unbeholden to anyone for their rights. Instead of hewing to religious dogma regarding fetuses, science must prevail. There is no basis in science to support the position that life begins at conception. Conception occurs in the Fallopian tube, requiring the fertilized egg to travel into the womb, a journey that can consume as much as five to seven days, and even more time before the egg can attach to the wall of the uterus. It is clear that life cannot begin, nor was it intended by nature to begin until the human egg attaches to and grows in the wall of the uterus. Failure to attach causes the fertilized egg to die and be swept out in the next menstrual cycle, an event that can correctly be called a natural abortion. Such events occur untold millions of times each year, without the knowledge of the females involved. We will require that all politicians and persons, including religious, within this country recognize these facts of life. The Federal Government will be prevented from applying dogmatic premises in all legislation throughout the land, and will be prevented from using such dogma in international relations with other lands.

We will free the American people from their long dependence on foreign oil, which in turn fuels our involvement in the Middle East. We will require all auto manufacturers to convert their vehicles to operate on alcohol or other alternative fuels. We will prevent oil companies from involving themselves in alcohol or other alternative fuel production and delivery to the public. Further, we will require all energy corporations to limit their activity to one fuel or energy source. No longer will huge energy- related corporations be able to be in oil, nuclear, coal, etc. Those which are already so involved will be required to divest all companies but one.

We will stop the runaway federal Judiciary from continuing to make new law. We will make it possible for Americans to take action against any federal or state judge that works against their best interests. We will put all judges in a Constitutional box from which they cannot again take some of the actions that they have taken in the past.

Finally, we will, as Abraham Lincoln said, dismember the federal Government and make it over to our satisfaction, or we will throw it off completely and start over. Our forefathers, the authors of the Declaration of Independence and the original Constitution, who made us Sovereigns, would expect no less from us. We have suffered long enough. This land is our land, and WE will run it.

Of course, the Government and those who have been in power since WW II will fight back, hoping to stop what must happen. They will leave no stone unturned to denigrate and smear every effort to change, and fight every effort to change what has been set in place over sixty years. Their great ally will be the leftist media, which is essentially a mouthpiece for the status quo, and the handmaiden of the powerful corporations behind the rotten policies that have plagued the people for more than half a century.

If we fight with determination, we will prevail, and the American people will be free once again, and with vigilance against those who would revert to the old system, for all time to come.

# ABOUT THE FUTURE

The Sovereign American intends to become a force for political change in the United States. But no one believes that this can become a reality without the active participation of hundreds of thousands of people who believe what the Sovereign American believes; that the Government must be changed to reflect what the American people want. This cannot be done without your help. The Sovereign American intends to become a political party to force Government to change. Your contributions are needed. Your e-mail addresses are needed. Let your voice be heard. Send contributions to The Sovereign American Association, Post Office Box 861, Deleon Springs, Florida, 32130. And thank you! Send e-mail to: editor@sovereignamerican.com.

# APPENDIX 1

## THE TRUTH ABOUT NUCLEAR WAR

By
H.L. Moxham
Copyright 2002

Because much has changed in the relationships between nations in recent years, and because there are now new dangers for the Republic, the following information is included in The Sovereign American. This data is not generally available to the public, although it is now unclassified. The source of this information was first published after WWII, and later revised to include the latest information. The title of this reference book is THE EFFECTS OF NUCLEAR WEAPONS, and was published by the Department of Defense.

Although this information originated in the 1950's it is still valid. The science of nuclear explosions has not changed much in the intervening years, but of course, weapon technology itself has greatly changed. Nevertheless, a nuclear explosion and its effects are still the same. This information, although incomplete, is of great concern to the average American and will be invaluable if this country is attacked with nuclear weapons. The most applicable data is included, but much complex mathematical and scientific data has been omitted. The remainder should not only be interesting, but it should be retained and preserved for your own safety.

Throughout the new Millennium, 1999 will be remembered as the year nuclear war again threatened the people of the United States. Through mismanagement of our nuclear weapons research facilities, compounded by near-treason on the part of corporate officials who should have known better, the Chinese military establishment was able to steal virtually every nuclear weapon secret possessed by the US.

Great damage has been done to our national security and will expose the American people to the danger of nuclear attack for decades. The Chinese Government and their military view the United States with great suspicion, envy and suppressed aggression. The North Koreans view us in the same way, and are very dangerous. Their proclivity for transferring weapons and data to other nations is well established. It will certainly transfer nuclear weapons information and their soon to be developed long range intercontinental missiles to its friends, which are universally antagonistic to the US. Iran, Libya, Iraq, etc. There can be little doubt as to their intentions in time of war. The United States will be their target.

It is almost certain that China, or North Korea, if they decide that the United States cannot be tolerated as the single superpower in the world, will form an axis with Iran, Iraq and Libya to combine their abilities to strike the US with nuclear-tipped missiles. While China and North Korea's present nuclear missile capabilities are limited, that will change, and when either China or North Korea decides to attack, their allies will be equipped with large numbers of Chinese or North Korean missiles and nuclear weapons as well. Reports indicate that China is building a 5000 mile range intercontinental missile delivery system, and the North Koreans are doing the same. China is expected to develop a 7000 mile range missile as well. With these missiles, much of the US will be within range and subject to attack.

Since WW II, the rest of the world has watched in awe as US war technology has established and reinforced its claim as a superpower. Even Europe, at the beginning of the millennium is recognizing its own war-making impotence in comparison to the US. And while the US has great military power and will be able to defend itself for at least a decade, there will come a time when the balance of nuclear power will shift to parity, and then superiority for the Chinese and her cohorts. North Korea will be close behind. As that time approaches, Washington will measure what is to be gained against what will be lost in a nuclear war with China or

North Korea and their axis partners. In those days, decisions made by high officials in Washington may not be the decisions the average American would make.

Indeed, the crop of politicians in Washington during the Clinton Administration made it abundantly clear that their decision might well be to surrender without firing a shot. It is highly questionable whether such politicians in the first decade of the new millennium will have the will-power to strike back at our attackers. China or North Korea and their allies will sense this weakness, and will attack massively to once and for all place the United States in an inferior position, prostrate and unable to oppose China's actions for many years.

With China or North Korea aligned with Iran, Iraq and Libya, and possibly with India or Pakistan, already nuclear powers, as well, the world order will be changed, The current president of Pakistan is constantly in danger of being assassinated or thrown out of office by internal forces more aligned with the old Government of Afghanistan than with the alliance with the US currently sponsored by the President of Pakistan.

And, India is facing a powerful sect in Kashmir that could revolt and shift India away from its friendly stance with America. If these two countries join the China-North Korea axis, the balance of power will be changed radically, perhaps forever. The world as proscribed by the globalists at the Council on Foreign Relations and Trilateral Commission will be turned upside down, and their ability to set things right through the military power of the United States will be completely destroyed.

An examination of a polar projection map of the world reveals why the United States may fall victim to a combined nuclear attack by its enemies. From Zizhiqi, in Manchuria it is 5000 Statute miles to Los Angeles, 6000 miles to Washington and 6800 miles to Miami, Florida, and North Korea is even closer to the United States. From Altay, in Tian Shan Province in China it is 6500 miles to Los Angeles, 6300 to Washington and 7300 to Miami. From

Tabriz, in Iran, it is 6000 miles to Washington and 6800 to Miami. From Tripoli, in Libya, it is 4800 miles to Washington and 5500 miles to Miami. Similar ranges from Pakistan and India can be determined if these countries join the others. By swinging these arcs across the United States, virtually every part of the country can be hit with nuclear warheads from each of those countries in a coordinated attack. If these countries decide to attack in concert, and each fires just ten ICBM's, the first strike will aim 70 missiles at the US. If they are MIRVed, with ten warheads apiece, seven hundred warheads will be aimed at the US. If Pakistan and India stay out, the total will be 50 missiles and 500 warheads.

The obvious answer to these attack capabilities is a robust anti-missile defense system, a system that can destroy incoming missiles and warheads and thus spare the American people the terrible fate that will otherwise befall them. But perverse thinking ( and perhaps a modicum of cowardice) on the part of high officials in Washington has until this year stopped all efforts to initiate a missile defense system for the American people. That is changing under the Bush Administration, certainly a step in the right direction. With the Chinese theft of our nuclear technology, there is no higher priority for the United States than a missile defense system. Yet many decry such a defense effort, saying that the task is an impossible one. That is not true. Forty-odd years ago, a program called Nike X successfully intercepted missile warheads fired from California at Kwajelain Island in the western pacific. This is not an insoluble problem.

So, what is the average person to do in the face of a potential nuclear attack by China or North Korea and her rogue state cohorts? How can one prepare for the terrible effects of nuclear explosions? Actually, quite a lot.

The first thing to understand is that no single nation, including the United States has ever fired the number of missiles at one time that would be required to completely disable the United States. Not even close. Second, any intercontinental missile must be maintained in a ready condition, or it may fail in its mission. Firing such a missile and achieving its trajectory is a very complicated task to undertake if the target is to be hit. A failure rate of at least 10 percent is likely under the best of conditions.

Accordingly, one out of ten missiles will fail, or 10 out of a hundred will never reach the intended target. Then there are duds; a nuclear warhead is a very complicated device. As many as another ten percent will impact the earth without exploding. Then there is such a thing as the Circular Error Probability. The missile may simply miss its target by as much as twenty miles over a long flight. This problem may affect the remaining 80 percent. Among this number a significant number may be destroyed due to the Anti-missile defense system.

And when the missile is launched, the warhead is not armed to prevent a nuclear explosion if the missile falls back on the country that launched it. This means that the warhead must arm itself in flight after it is safely launched. As many as another 10 percent may not arm properly. And finally, as soon as the first launch is detected by the United States, which is to say immediately, there will be as much as 30 minutes or more before the first warhead will explode, and in that 30 minutes, US retaliatory strikes will decimate the launching country and additional launches are quite problematical. The entire first strike plan may well be truncated or even forestalled. As many as 50 percent of the missiles to be fired may be destroyed during the retaliatory response. The Anti-Missile Defense System should be able to handle the rest. If the attacking countries do not get off their first strike completely, they will never fire another missile at the US. They will be destroyed before they can be set up and armed.

But nothing in war is certain. Now it can be seen why the President has insisted that the Anti- Missile Defense System go forward. As the years march by this system will improve until a high percentage of the attacking missiles will be destroyed.

Even so, there are other mitigating factors. Wherever the warheads may fall, the effects of nuclear explosions are not omnipresent; there are finite limits to those effects and with knowledge, millions of Americans can do much to ensure their survival. The effects of nuclear explosions are terrible if you are close to them and unprepared. Very few people survive at ground zero. But the farther you are from ground zero, the less the effects. Even fairly close to ground zero, survival is possible if precautions are taken. Remember, the effects, heat and blast, of such an explosion are rapidly spread over large distances, each forming its own front in a perfect circle, with expansion away from ground zero along all points of the circle. That expansion progressively reduces the weapon effect each second it moves away from ground zero.

The sequence of events of all nuclear explosions are the same, and will occur in sequence. Light, heat, blast and sometimes fallout. Because the light of the nuclear explosion is essentially harmless unless viewed directly by the human eye, this effect will be ignored. It is sufficient to recall that of the two explosions in Japan in 1945, not one case of permanent blindness was recorded. Virtually all cases of temporary blindness cleared up in hours.

The heat pulse of the explosion is caused by the rapid development of the fireball as well as other factors. Heat is the most dangerous to humans because protection must be sought as soon as the light from an explosion is seen. Still, even light, white clothing can provide some protection, but any solid object, such as a piece of plywood, can shield you from heat pulse burns. The plywood will char and perhaps ignite, but you will have been protected in the meantime. The heat pulse will last for a few moments, then quickly dissipate. Remember that the plywood will not protect you from the blast front which will quickly follow the heat pulse. You should also understand that the heat pulse does not heat the atmosphere except very close to the fireball, so there will not be a change in the ambient air temperature around you.

There are two kinds of nuclear explosions: a ground burst, and an air burst. Ground bursts are much less effective; air bursts are the most effective from a military standpoint. Therefore, it can be expected that air bursts will be used in most cases. What can be expected from either explosion? First, at the moment of the explosion, an intense white light is produced. This light, the whitest light ever seen by man, is harmless, even near ground zero. Unless it is viewed directly or concentrated by magnification (as with field glasses) the light is insignificant as a weapon effect.

Within a very few seconds, the white light fades and is supplanted by the explosion and fireball. The fireball grows rapidly and will cause burns, and charring of painted surfaces. However, this is radiated heat (as from a fireplace) and can easily be evaded by stepping behind a large tree trunk or wall. Any solid structure will do. The fireball will last for several seconds, depending on the warhead yield (explosive force). For those indoors, burns will not be a factor, but windows should be avoided since glass will simply transmit the heat energy. Metal venetian blinds or screens will suffice to stop the heat pulse, but exposed curtains may ignite and burn. Everyone should have metal venetian blinds or screens on their windows.

Within additional seconds, the blast front will arrive and will be very destructive near ground zero. The farther away from ground zero, the less destructive the blast front will be. After the blast front passes, a surge of air back toward ground zero will follow, but this air movement will not be destructive in nature. Most injuries from blast will be caused by flying objects or collapsing structures or by the individual being blown against solid objects such as a wall or other structure. Those inside at the time of the blast should stay away from windows because the window opening will concentrate the blast, and injuries from flying glass and other debris will result.

And to put an old myth to rest for once and all, there was no evidence at either Hiroshima or Nagasaki that anyone had been vaporized. It simply didn't happen. Lurid scenes in some movies showing people with their skeletons visible as in an x-ray were simply figments of a screenwriter's imagination. It is always wise to remember that the subject of nuclear weapons has been propagandized unmercifully by the anti-nuclear war activists ever since the end of WW II. Many of their views were simply false. A prime example of such falsities was the infamous "nuclear winter" prediction, for which there never was substantive technical or scientific evidence.

The next thing to understand is that in the photographs of Hiroshima and Nagasaki, the destroyed Japanese cities that were attacked at the end of WW II, are not representative of American cities which might be attacked by the Chinese or North Korea and her allies. Japanese cities of 1945 were largely made of wood and paper, with only a few buildings constructed of steel and reinforced concrete. Japanese houses were notoriously flimsy and counterparts cannot be found in US cities. In fact, there were no counterparts of such houses in American cities even in 1945. The effects of nuclear explosions over US cities will not produces hundreds of square miles of leveled areas consisting of ashes as in Hiroshima and Nagasaki, unless it is a suburb hit by many explosions.

This does not mean that there will not be blast damage and fires; there will be. But it does mean that blast and fires will be much less effective in destroying US cities than was the case in Japan. Most central city areas in US cities will be damaged but most reasonably modern buildings will stand and not collapse. Most will have their windows blown out and the structure damaged, but at a reasonable distance ( .6 Miles or 3150 Ft.) from the explosion the structure should survive. Remember, no modern city has ever been struck by a nuclear explosion; predictions of damage from blast and fire, no matter who makes them, are based upon fifty year old test data and are highly conjectural when applied to modern cities and structures. Significantly, the 1950's tests did not include a representative city constructed for test purposes.

Nevertheless, the possibility of a nuclear attack on the US means that as many people as possible must evacuate from target cities and seek refuge in smaller towns and the countryside. That means that each person must prepare for such action and take as much survival equipment with him as possible. Preplanning the evacuation is a must, and each person must know where he plans to relocate temporarily. Estimates of the time when China or North Korea and her allies might decide to attack are very subjective, but it is thought that a decade or more will pass before that decision will be taken. Prudence dictates that Americans in target areas should use that decade to prepare for evacuation, and have specific locations in mind or established and prepared for use. In making that decision, special attention must be given to factors outlined in the following paragraphs.

It is important to understand an additional fact about nuclear explosions. If the fireball from an airburst touches the ground, it will suck up hundreds, perhaps thousands of tons of debris and dust, which will result in fallout in the form of ash. The amount of debris picked up by the fireball depends on the size of the fireball, which is a function of the yield of the warhead. The larger the fireball, the more fallout can be expected.

All fallout will be radioactive and dangerous. It must be avoided. How? Simple. The fireball rises at about 300 miles per hour and will not slow down until it reaches the stratosphere or about 60-80,000 ft altitude. At that altitude, in the northern hemisphere, prevailing winds are from west to east. The heavier debris particles will fall out fastest, and will reach the ground downwind from ground zero about 30-40 minutes after an explosion.

There are two kinds of fallout. That which is carried into the stratosphere, about 80,000 to 120,000 feet, by an air burst, and that which rises to a maximum of about 30,000 feet, as from a surface burst. They are both similar but require different calculations to determine their range and radioactivity.

If you witness a nuclear explosion to the north of your position, you would not flee east, but rather, to the south or west. If, in the worst case, you notice a nuclear explosion to the west, you must flee to the north or south, as fast as possible. Wind speeds at altitude can be great, so fleeing east would simply let the fallout overtake your evacuation.

If in doubt about which way to flee, simply move as rapidly as possible away from the eastward path of the cloud. The safest location in the United States from fallout from distant explosions is the southwest coast of Florida from roughly Cedar Key to Naples. Because there are almost no strategic targets in that area, it should be free of nuclear explosions as well. The US west coast would be free from explosions to the west, but there are so many targets along the coast of western states that evacuation will be required.

Most fallout will have a relatively short half-life, which means that its radioactivity will decay fairly rapidly. Protection from more intense levels must be sought in the deepest levels of large buildings or in caves. For smaller explosions and less intense radiation a reasonably safe shelter can also be fashioned from a pit covered with logs or lumber which in turn are also covered with as much earth as possible without endangering its occupants from collapse. Even on the surface, a person standing against a concrete wall is exposed to much less fallout radiation than he would be if standing in the middle of a street intersection. Moving rapidly to a shelter of some kind, even a frame house, will provide considerable protection.

Refuge in a shelter for 3-6 days should be expected, and the necessary food, water and sanitary equipment must be provided. These can be as rudimentary as necessary to get through the fallout period. Unless you have a radiation monitor (Geiger counter or dosimeter) you will have to depend on radio reports about the radiation level in your area before leaving the shelter. Refer to the fallout pattern charts to estimate the danger to you at your location in relation to targets that may be struck by a nuclear explosion. (There are many scientific and mathematical formulas applicable to the subject of fallout and are not explored here.)

Realistically, one can only generalize the distribution and patterns of fallout after an explosion, or series of explosions. The best plan of action is probably to try to flee to the south and west of any position in the northeast or midwest, but other explosions in your path may require other movements. Generally speaking, movement to the east will be least effective in seeking protection, except on the west coast where little other choice is available. Monitoring of the radio for news of other explosions and fallout areas will be extremely important during this time.

There is no substitute for preplanning your safety in the event of a nuclear attack. But it should be remembered that millions of people in the US live in non-target areas, and in each case, they should prepare a basement or other shelter which will provide all the fallout protection needed. For those in urban areas, the actions to be taken are more complex but certainly not impossible. Leave a safe shelter only when you know that the radiation level outside is safe. If rain falls in your area after you have taken refuge from fallout, the radioactive particles and ash will wash into low areas and cause a radioactive "hot spot" which should be avoided when you exit the shelter. Your fallout shelter should not be built in a low spot.

If the fireball remains well above the surface of the earth, fallout will be negligible. In both explosions over Japan in 1945, fallout was nonexistent because the fireballs remained well above the earth. At Hiroshima, the explosion was detonated at 1670 ft, with a yield of about 12.5 kilotons, and at Nagasaki, the explosion was at 1640 ft, with a yield of 22 kilotons. (Kiloton=thousands of tons of high explosives; Megaton=millions of tons of high explosives.)

This entire picture will be altered and confused when there are multiple strikes against cities, industrial or urban areas, and the best possible protection and actions must be decided upon in each case. But civilians in the target area should leave the vicinity as soon as possible. A distance of twenty miles is the least necessary, and twice that is highly desirable when evacuating around an explosion site. Never evacuate to the east of an explosion site.

Remember, no one actually knows what will happen in a massive nuclear attack. For instance, where fires may be started by an early warhead, later warhead explosions may actually extinguish fires started by the first warhead. Some warheads will be wasted by repeated attacks on already destroyed areas, and some warheads will fail to detonate. Every war has its share of unexploded ordnance and nuclear warheads are subject to a greater than average failure rate due to their complex construction and precise requirements for fusing, etc.

Nuclear weapons are fused by radar, and will detonate at the programmed altitude over the target. If the warhead fails to explode, it will impact in the target area and bury itself as much as 150 ft. underground. The US has no present capability or trained personnel to locate and disarm such warheads, and a large area around unexploded warheads will have to be evacuated until it is safe for people to return to the site. This area will also include a fallout zone because if the armed warhead suddenly explodes a huge amount of dirt will be thrown into the air and spread downwind from the warhead penetration site. Because a new incoming warhead is fused by radar, the radar my detect the dirt cloud from a surface burst and cause the warhead to explode far above its intended altitude, reducing its effects at ground level.

Some people will observe that it is futile to try to prepare for survival in the event of a nuclear attack, that there will not be time to evacuate to the countryside away from target cities, etc. That may not be the case at all. A potential enemy state planning to attack the US has a variety of problems that make the task seem daunting. First, no country on earth has ever launched the number of missiles that would be required for a massive first strike. Very few have the capability to do so. But in the event that the attack is actually undertaken, it must involve more than one country so that the combined number of missiles will have the best possibility of success. The more likely scenario would expect that the attack would be sustained over a period of several days, with periods of inactivity that can be used for evacuation out of any target areas. Such an attack should be completed and missiles exhausted in a week.

But no country has yet been able to control the weather to ensure optimum conditions at the target. On any given day, clouds and rain can be present in large areas while others are clear. There were no tests conducted to determine the mitigating effect of weather on the effectiveness of nuclear weapons. In fact all tests were conducted in the western US with very clear weather conditions so that photographic records could be made of the explosion and its effect on certain buildings, autos, military equipment, etc. could be studied in the laboratory.

Accordingly, no one knows whether the fireball will ignite or even char wooden structures if the structure has been subjected to several hours or days of rain. It is virtually certain that roofs which had been soaked by rain will not ignite as easily as dry roofs otherwise would. The effect of haze or fog, or low clouds is unknown. Yet these conditions will all work to degrade the effects of nuclear blasts. Calculations of such conditions on the effects of nuclear explosions were made, but involved theoretical values. No empirical data was ever developed. The more clouds and rain that are present at the time of an attack, the more the destructive effects of the nuclear explosion will be attenuated. The effect of a snow covered terrain, for example, is to reflect heat upward, reducing the effect at ground level.

The most likely scenario to take place when the attack begins is that some cities will be hit first, with others to be hit later. Washington and New York will be the first, and hit hard by multiple strikes since the enemy will want to decapitate the Government and thus stop retaliatory orders sent to our own forces. It will, however, not affect the effort to strike the enemy. Our nuclear missile forces and submarines will see to that.

After the first cities are hit, the news will quickly spread nationwide and many people will have time to leave their homes and evacuate. Because of the number of missiles and warheads required to destroy the US ability to fight, several days may be available for evacuations to continue. No nation on earth has the ability to move great numbers of people in time of need as does the US. Hurricanes routinely cause hundreds of thousands of coastal residents to evacuate to safe areas within hours. With as much as several days available, millions of people can be moved to safer areas. How they survive after relocation will be a major problem, but with preplanning, life will go on. Do not depend on the Government for help, the problem will be too great for effective assistance to be provided. Take care of yourself.

In addition, it is by no means certain that MIRVed (Multiple Independently Targeted Reentry Vehicle) warheads will separate from their boost vehicle (bus) at the apogee of the ballistic trajectory, and in no way certain that they will acquire their own individual, precise and different trajectories to hit their separate targets. Thus in an attack against Los Angeles, for instance, warheads may detonate over Catalina Island instead of at their precise aiming points in the Los Angeles area.

If there can be any good aspect of the Chinese theft of our nuclear weapons information, it is that the US arsenal of warheads and bombs has for many years been gradually reduced in yield. That is, there has been a deliberate plan to reduce the blast potential of such weapons because missile accuracy has been refined to the point where larger (multi-megaton) yields are wasteful. Pinpoint accuracy of bombing in Kosovo and Serbia has, along with the Gulf War, and Iraqi war, demonstrated that bombing can be effectively conducted with a minimum of damage to areas near the target.

The day of multi-megaton weapons has passed. While China is thought to have a missile with a multi-megaton warhead it is thought that their own nuclear warhead arsenal will also undergo a modernization similar to that of the US, where smaller yields are better, especially if missile accuracy improves as well. (The technical means to ensure missile accuracy was provided to the Chinese by an American civilian Contractor.) Nuclear weapons are extremely expensive and China and North Korea too, will decide that less is more where these weapons are concerned. As far as is known, North Korea has never attempted to build a large yield warhead.

Some people have observed that small nuclear weapons the size of a valise can be smuggled into the US easily, and that is true. These are known as demolition munitions. Such weapons have existed in the US arsenal in the past, but their use by a potential enemy state bent on conducting a major attack on the US is not feasible. Such an attack would be feeble indeed. But a real attack with missiles would possibly entail the use of weapons from the size used at Hiroshima and Nagasaki, to possibly a 1 megaton warhead. That means the explosions will range from 10 kilotons to 1 megaton ( one millions tons of TNT). The fireballs will range in size from about a hundred yards to 5700 feet ( 1.1 miles) across.

One last item must be remembered about nuclear weapons and that is that they all emit an electromagnetic pulse (EMP) when they explode. This effect is not harmful to humans, but it can cripple or destroy sensitive electronic equipment, including computers. A deliberate attempt to knock out the electronic/electrical systems in the US might be made. It is sufficient to know that the essential military equipment has been shielded and hardened against EMP, and their equipment will not be affected. As for civilians, if it happens there is nothing you can do about such an attack. If you have trouble with your TV or radio, EMP probably is responsible.

The Chinese or North Korea and its rogue clients will attack suddenly and without warning, as the Japanese did in 1941 at Pearl Harbor. Surprise is a necessary element of any plan to defeat the US militarily. But with preparation, much of the attack can be blunted, and reprisal attacks launched against the Chinese mainland, North Korea or any other country. It should be recognized, however that the US cannot use nuclear weapons against invaders who are able to reach the US proper. In the Aleutian Islands, yes, and even in parts of Alaska, too. But such attacks will put at hazard our friends in Canada due the easterly movement of fallout. Preparations must be made to hit the invaders hard in the Aleutians and western Alaska, and stop them in those remote areas. Canadians, with adequate preparation, can survive the fallout.

The United States is a huge nation, and no combination of outside nations can actually defeat us. They can cause great physical and economic damage, and kill many people, but this Nation has recovered after a major civil war, with more than 600,000 dead, and now possesses more with which to recover from such an attack than any other nation on earth. Our enemies, on the other hand, will live and die in their radioactive rubble for many generations.

# APPENDIX 2

## AFTER THE ATTACK
## HOW DO WE SURVIVE?

### By
### Howard. L. Moxham
### Copyright 2003

The information contained in this Appendix is intended to complement that found in Appendix I.

You can survive a nuclear attack. Your survival is virtually assured if you live in a rural area not near a major city or a target area, such as an operating military installation or a major airport with much air traffic. Millions of people in the United States do not live in a target area. Nevertheless, you must prepare for fallout in any case. Fallout can kill you if you are exposed to it for a long period of time. For the rest, survival depends on your ability to take care of yourself. If you live in a target area, and the attack has not arrived, you will have to evacuate as soon as possible. The following paragraphs will help.

The best estimate of the time of year that the enemy will make their attack is in late spring or early summer. Why? In the winter the weather factors are such that a great many effects of nuclear explosions will be attenuated or diminished on the ground. In spring there is too much rain, and too many clouds, which also works to diminish nuclear explosion effects. That leaves late spring, summer and fall. Roughly a week of May, all of June and July, all of August and all of September. Possibly most of October. A total of about 155 days. It will be about six to ten years before China and North Korea will have enough warheads and missiles to feel bold enough to make the strike and line up their cohorts. Probably 2009 to 2013, give or take a couple of years.

Choose your evacuation destination well in advance. Pick your destination carefully. It should be able to sustain you in every respect after you arrive, and be secure from attack. It does no good to go from target to target. Most likely you have knowledge of a vacation area that can meet your needs.

Others will pick it as well, so don't be surprised by the presence of others when you arrive. If you will be renting a home or other residence, call ahead or have a permanent arrangement with the owner. Make sure he knows you are coming, and that you will occupy the residence until the emergency is over. Be prepared to fend off others if the evacuation is a major one, and the local area is overwhelmed. Guard your supplies. Have someone in the residence at all times, and preferably equipped with a radio that can keep you advised of local conditions in your absence.

What to do first. Plan and prepare. Plan your escape route out of the area. Know which Interstates you will take. WARNING! your escape will be hindered by millions of other attempting to do the same thing. The Interstates will quickly be overloaded. Expect delays of hours and plan your actions. Know alternative routes and be prepared to take them. Do not travel alone if possible. A small caravan is desirable. Even two vehicles are better than traveling alone. Keep in radio contact with the others by CB radio. DO NOT DISCUSS YOUR PLANS OR CONDITION ON THE RADIO.

For a small caravan, it is wise to have a single (pathfinder) vehicle traveling on your route several miles ahead, but close enough to maintain radio contact. That vehicle can alert you to actions being taken by the authorities which you might want to avoid. If, for instance, you are advised by your pathfinder vehicle that the authorities are confiscating weapons which you might need, go around that roadblock. The pathfinder vehicle can rejoin you later. DO NOT DISCUSS THIS ON THE RADIO. Have your actions preplanned in such an event.

Maintain your vehicle. Always have reasonably new tires on your vehicle. Make sure they are inflated to the proper tire pressure every two weeks. Replace any tire that seems to have defects. If you have an RV or SUV, get one with an extra fuel tank. (This will not be easy, but if you are ordering a new vehicle, it might be possible to get an extra fuel tank.) Make sure the vehicle is at least one half full of fuel at any given time. The fuel range (miles) of your car should be as great as possible before refueling is necessary. Gas stations will be inundated with refugees. Know how far you can travel on a full fuel tank. That is the range you can expect. Plan to drive as long as possible without stopping in the first hours of an attack. Use a portapotty for relief. Carry the food you will need. Do not drive until your fuel is exhausted. Begin looking for a filling station well ahead of that point and refuel fully. If the battery in your vehicle is a year and a half old, replace it. You do not need a failing battery to disable your vehicle at this time. Most batteries will need to be replaced at two years anyway. Don't take a chance.

Your vehicle, particularly if it is a SUV or other one which the interior can easily viewed from the outside, should have well tinted windows. Observation of your passengers and supplies is not what you want at this time. Get your windows tinted. Privacy is paramount.

Stay in the United States. Do not cross the border into Mexico. You may be in more danger there than anyplace in the US. Canada may seem to be a refuge, but fallout may be worse there than in many areas of the US. In the US, information will be broadcast on every radio and TV station or network. Help will be available sooner in the US and in more locations.

Food and necessities. Most outdoors stores, sporting goods stores, Gun shops, etc., can tell you where to get magazines that will have advertisements for freeze dried foods that you can stock up on. These are invaluable in an emergency. Since they are freeze dried, they contain little moisture and thus are light weight. Most are foil packed and will last for about five years. Preparation is simple. Just add water and heat. They can be eaten cold. Many companies offer very tasty varieties of such foods. (Suggestion- buy from suppliers in and around Salt Lake City, Utah. The Mormons have a long history and experience with storage foods.) Be sure to maintain a supply of fresh batteries for your small radio or portable TV. Keep the receipts and check them yearly to make sure they are not nearing their expiration dates. If they are, replace them. Make sure your CB radio is working every six months. If it is more than three years old, replace it. INFORMATION WHILE YOU ARE TRAVELING IS YOUR MOST IMPORTANT TOOL! Preparing for an evacuation is exactly like preparing to evacuate away from a hurricane. Take everything you can and don't expect to replace supplies easily. Other people will soon exhaust supplies no matter where you go. Try to depend on food that requires no refrigeration. You can buy a portable cooler that is electric and runs off your car battery. It will help to keep sodas cold and will make life less daunting on your journey. Finally, prepare to use only paper plates and plastic cups. Dispose of them as soon as possible. You do not need to live among piles of trash at any time. Your sense of well-being will be better off if you can display your control of the situation in these difficult times.

Toilet necessities. Stock up on a variety of plastic bags. They can be used as a toilet in an emergency, and are easily disposed of. Stock up on toilet paper. Towelettes are handy and some are moisturized or medicated. Your natural instincts will dictate what you need for personal hygiene. Make sure these things are in sufficient supply to last for several months.

Other tips. Carry sufficient cash or travelers checks for your needs, but keep them hidden. Large bills, more than 50.00 should be avoided. Have a tailor sew a money pocket inside the belt line of your trousers. Use a money belt for your reserve cash. Do not flash your money at any time. If you need to spend several bills, take them out of your pocket ahead of time and hold them in your closed fist before your purchase. You may not be able to use your credit cards. Local stores in rural or semi-rural areas may insist on cash for your purchases. This will almost certainly happen if their supplies run low. Avoid single men, or groups of men in camp areas. Camp with friends when possible. DO NOT DISCUSS YOUR CIRCUMSTANCES WITH THOSE YOU DO NOT KNOW. Do not attract attention in such areas. STAY TOGETHER.

Trust your instincts. Read the news or listen to the radio or TV as much as possible and keep up to date. If your instincts tell you that an attack is imminent, leave as soon as possible. Your survival and well being may be assured by a few hours of advance travel. You may be able to travel more in five hours of advance movement than you could in five times that much time after an attack is announced.

Monitor the radio or portable TV. Nothing is more important than accurate information when you travel. Be well aware of the other explosions in your area, (within fifty miles) which may endanger you. Calculate the fallout movement and travel accordingly. Radio stations will be on the air constantly updating you with the latest information. Alter your travel as necessary to avoid the newest danger. On a reasonably clear day or night, you will be able to see the flash of a nuclear explosion and the rising fireball and cloud. If it is to your right ahead of you, do not pass it to the left, which will be in the path of the fallout as the cloud moves east. DO NOT APPROACH THE TARGET AREA, Travel to the right(west) and keep the location of the explosion on your left until you pass it by a wide margin. Then turn to the left if you wish to travel further to the south.

Practice your evacuation. Every chance you get, at least once a year, you should combine your vacation with a practice evacuation. Leave with everything you would need and drive as far as you can without stopping. Do not exceed the speed limit; (you will not be able to speed in a real evacuation.) Eat on the fly, and use a portapotty as necessary. Practice makes perfect and you will need the experience. Have a destination in mind and note how easy or difficult it is to make the trip. Make sure that your destination will be what you want in an emergency. Make this trip several times in the same manner. It will be worth the trouble.

If we are to face a nuclear attack, take a tip from our British cousins, who, during WW II when London was being bombed during the Blitz of 1940, evacuated their children to the countryside. If you have relatives or grandparents living in an area that is not considered a target area, consider taking your children there for the duration of the emergency. Your peace of mind will be comforting, even though you are separated temporarily.

How big will the weapons be? It's a guess, but it's almost certain that the largest will be about 1 megaton, and that will come from China. Most attacking warheads will be between 50 and 150 kiloton. The attacking nations will not want to waste their fissionable material. They know they cannot knock us out of the war, but they will want to cause as much economic damage as possible. That they can do. And kill a large number of people. The affect on our economy will be very serious, but we can recover. And in ten years our population will be back where it was before the war. Remember, 600,000 men died in the Civil War. We survived as a people and moved on. We will survive this. On the other hand, our enemies will not have a viable economy for a CENTURY or more. We will hope that their survivors will learn that they cannot defeat us. Their ancestors, like the Japanese, died trying.

# APPENDIX 3

## SUPPORTING DATA

**By**
**H.L. Moxham**
**Copyright 2003**

The following charts, graphs and photographs are intended to support some of the material in the preceding Appendixes. Space does not permit the inclusion of much more data, which is available. However, since this document was never intended to be a text book, the materials included will provide a basic understanding of the subjects covered.

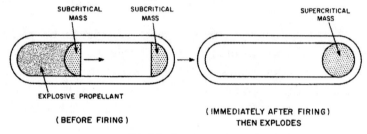

Principle of a gun-assembly nuclear device.

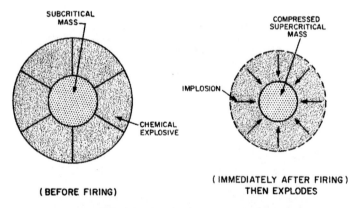

Principle of an implosion-type nuclear device.

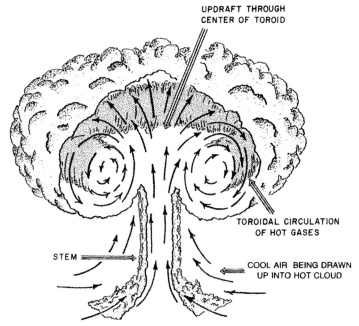

UPDRAFT THROUGH
CENTER OF TOROID

TOROIDAL CIRCULATION
OF HOT GASES

STEM

COOL AIR BEING DRAWN
UP INTO HOT CLOUD

Cutaway showing artist's conception of toroidal circulation within the
radioactive cloud from a nuclear explosion.

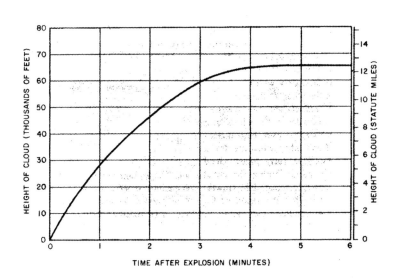

### Table 2.12
**RATE OF RISE OF RADIOACTIVE CLOUD**
**FROM A 1-MEGATON AIR BURST**

| Height (miles) | Time (minutes) | Rate of Rise (miles per hour) |
|:---:|:---:|:---:|
| 2 | 0.3 | 330 |
| 4 | 0.7 | 270 |
| 6 | 1.1 | 220 |
| 10 | 2.5 | 140 |
| 12 | 3.8 | 27 |

**GENERAL PRINCIPLES OF NUCLEAR EXPLOSIONS**

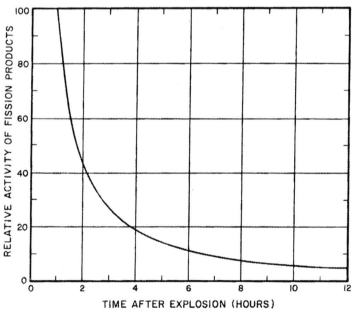

Rate of Decay of fission products after a nuclear explosion (activity is taken as 100 at 1 hour after the detonation).

131

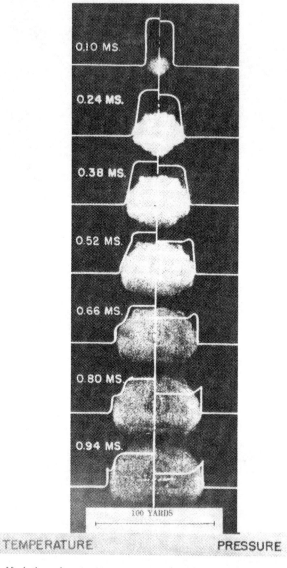

0.10 MS.

0.24 MS.

0.38 MS.

0.52 MS.

0.66 MS.

0.80 MS.

0.94 MS.

100 YARDS

TEMPERATURE

PRESSURE

Variation of temperature and pressure in the fireball.

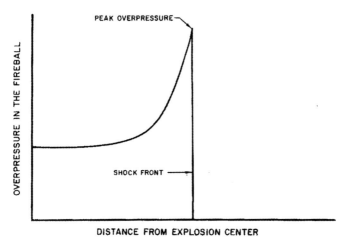

DISTANCE FROM EXPLOSION CENTER

Figure 3.03. Variation of overpressure with distance in the fireball.

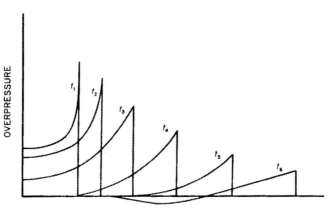

DISTANCE FROM EXPLOSION

Variation of overpressure in air with distance at successive times.

PEAK OVERPRESSURE AND DYNAMIC PRESSURE AND MAXIMUM WIND VELOCITY
IN AIR AT SEA LEVEL CALCULATED FOR AN IDEAL SHOCK FRONT

| Peak overpressure (pounds per square inch) | Peak dynamic pressure (pounds per square inch) | Maximum wind velocity (miles per hour) |
| --- | --- | --- |
| 200 | 330 | 2,078 |
| 150 | 222 | 1,777 |
| 100 | 123 | 1,415 |
| 72 | 74 | 1,168 |
| 50 | 41 | 934 |
| 30 | 17 | 669 |
| 20 | 8.1 | 502 |
| 10 | 2.2 | 294 |
| 5 | 0.6 | 163 |
| 2 | 0.1 | 70 |

133

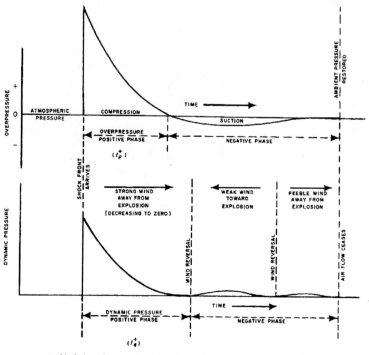

Variation of overpressure and dynamic pressure with time at a fixed location.

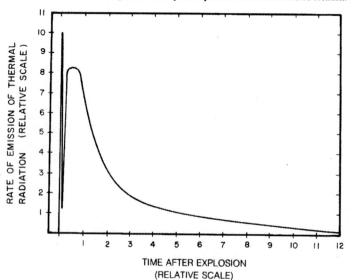

TIME AFTER EXPLOSION
(RELATIVE SCALE)

Upper photo: Reinforced-concrete, aseimic structure; window fire shutters were blown in by blast and the interior gutted by fire (0.12 mile from ground zero at Hiroshima). Lower photo: Burned out interior of similar structure.

Figure 5.52.  Upper photo; Wood-frame building; 1.0 mile from ground zero at Hiroshima. Lower photo: Frame of residence under construction, showing small tenons.

Figure 5.73. Reinforced precast concrete house after a nuclear explosion (5 psi peak overpressure). The LP-gas tank, sheltered by the house, is essentially undamaged.

Figure 5.76. Reinforced masonry-block house before a nuclear explosion, Nevada Test Site.

Figure 5.77. Reinforced masonry-block house after a nuclear explosion (5 psi peak overpressure).

Figure 5.102a.   Collapsed suspension tower (5 psi peak overpressure, 0.6 psi dynamic pressure from 30-kiloton explosion), Nevada Test Site.

Figure 5.102b.   Dead-end tower, suspension tower, and transformers (5 psi peak overpressure, 0.6 psi dynamic pressure from 30-kiloton explosion), Nevada Test Site. The trucks at the left of the photograph are those in Figure 5.89.

Figure 5.20b.  Three-story, reinforced-concrete frame building; walls were 13-inch thick brick panel with large window openings (0.13 mile from ground zero at Hiroshima).

Figure 5.127a  Bridge with deck of reinforced concrete on steel-plate girders; outer girder had concrete facing (270 feet from ground zero at Hiroshima). The railing was blown down but the deck received little damage so that traffic continued.

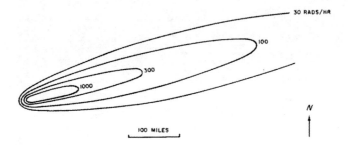

Figure 9.100a.   Idealized unit-time reference dose-rate contours for a 10-megaton, 50-percent fission, surface burst (30 mph effective wind speed).

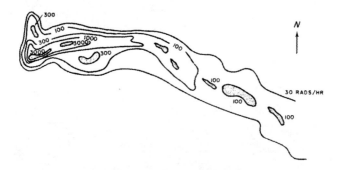

Figure 9.100b.   Corresponding actual dose-rate contours (hypothetical).

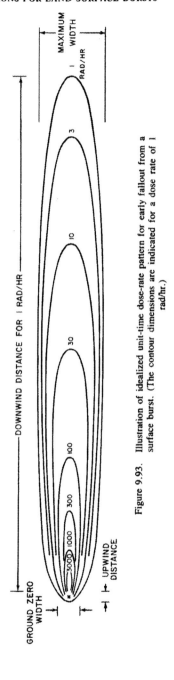

Figure 9.93.  Illustration of idealized unit-time dose-rate pattern for early fallout from a surface burst. (The contour dimensions are indicated for a dose rate of 1 rad/hr.)

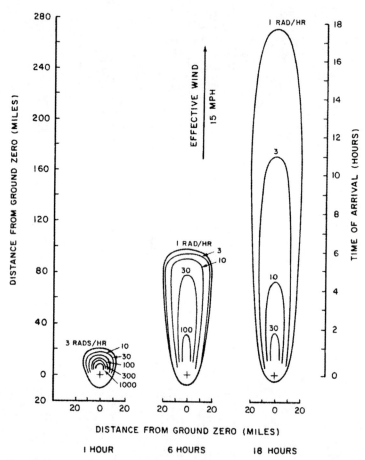

Figure 9.86a. Dose-rate contours from early fallout at 1, 6, and 18 hours after a surface burst with a total yield of 2 megatons and 1 megaton fission yield (15 mph effective wind speed).

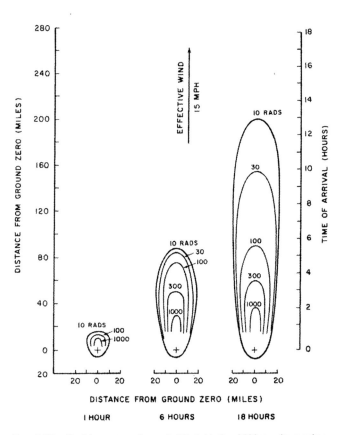

Figure 9.86b.   Total-dose contours from early fallout at 1, 6, and 18 hours after a surface burst with a total yield of 2 megatons and 1-megaton fission yield (15 mph effective wind speed).

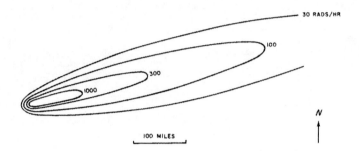

Figure 9.100a.  Idealized unit-time reference dose-rate contours for a 10-megaton, 50-per-cent fission, surface burst (30 mph effective wind speed).

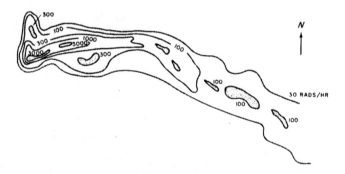

Corresponding actual dose-rate contours (hypothetical).

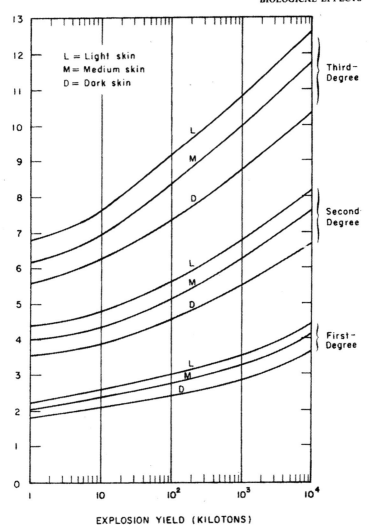

Radiant exposure required to produce skin burns for different skin pigmentations.

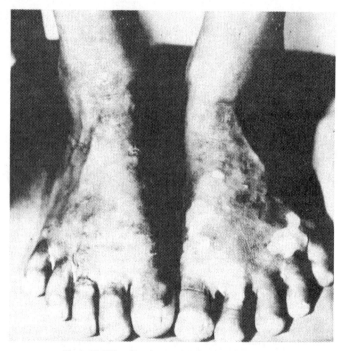

Figure 12.158b.  Beta burn on feet 1 month after exposure.

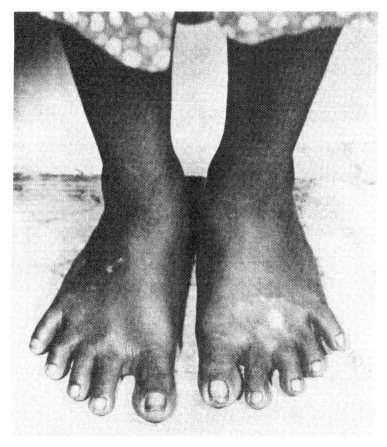

Figure 12.161b.   Beta burn on feet 6 months after exposure (see Fig. 12.158b).

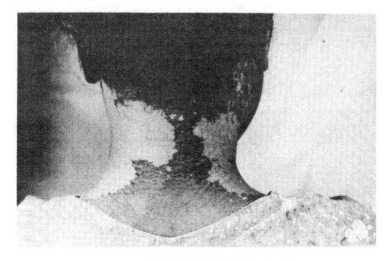

Beta burn on neck 1 month after exposure.

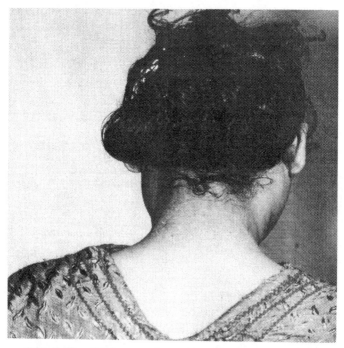

Figure 12.161a.   Beta burn on neck 1 year after exposure (see Fig. 12.158a).

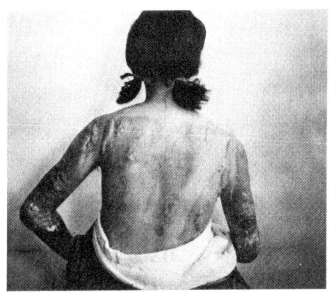

The skin under the areas of contact with clothing is burned. The protective effect of thicker layers can be seen on the shoulders and across the back.

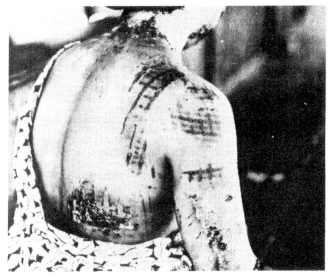

Figure 12.72. The patient's skin is burned in a pattern corresponding to the dark portions of a kimono worn at the time of the explosion

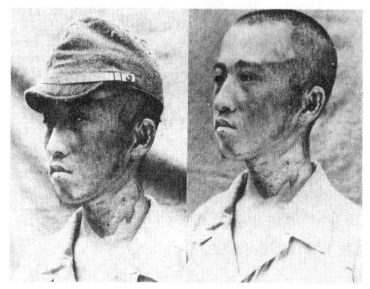

Partial protection against thermal radiation produced "profile" burns (1.23 miles from ground zero in Hiroshima; the radiant exposure was estimated to be 5.5 to 6 cal/cm²). The cap was sufficient to protect the top of the head against flash burn.